REJUVENATION

REJUVENATION

A WELLNESS GUIDE FOR WOMEN AND MEN

Horst Rechelbacher

HEALING ARTS PRESS
ROCHESTER, VERMONT

Healing Arts Press
One Park Street
Rochester, Vermont 05767

Library of Congress Cataloging-in-Publication Data

Rechelbacher, Horst.
    Rejuvenation : a wellness guide for women and men / by Horst Rechelbacher.
        p.   cm.
    Bibliography: p.
    Includes index.
    ISBN 0-89281-248-6 (pbk.)
    1. Rejuvenation. 2. Mind and body. 3. Beauty, Personal.
I. Title.
RA776.75.R43   1988
613—dc19   88-23531
                                                                                      CIP

Printed and bound in the United States

10 9 8 7 6 5 4

Healing Arts Press is a division of Inner Traditions International, Ltd.

Distributed to the book trade in the United States by Harper and Row Publishers, Inc.

Distributed to the book trade in Canada by Book Center, Inc., Montreal, Quebec

Distributed to the health food trade in Canada by Alive Books, Toronto and Vancouver

"Give me freedom to fly without a shadow.
Give me freedom to sing without an echo,
and to love without leaving traces."

— *Irina Tweedie*

This book is dedicated to my mother who, during her eighty-one years, used the gifts of nature, such as herbs, to nourish the body.

I humbly thank my teacher, H.H. Swami Rama, whose guidance and inspiration motivated me to adopt a lifestyle of physical and mental wellness.

I would like to give recognition and thanks to four talented spirits who contributed much time and love to this book:

Elizabeth Fink
Susan Mesner
Anne Morrow
Kiran Stordalen

Also many thanks for the support and contributions given by Dr. Phil Nuernberger and Dr. Alan Hymes.

Thanks to Ron Pulju for the beautiful illustrations.

And finally, a special thanks to my teacher Swami Rama for the motivation to write this book.

❦ Contents

❦ FOREWORD

AGE AND BEAUTY, a universal condition forever linked to a universal concern. Yet few in our modern society understand either. Most often age is understood as the natural enemy of beauty, and we speak fearfully of the ravages of time. But it is not age that is the enemy, rather ourselves, the habits of our personality, and our lack of understanding of ourselves, aging, and beauty that are so destructive to our natural beauty.

Traditionally, aging has been associated with serenity, wisdom, and fulfillment; seen as part of the natural order of things, the completion of life, and a time of preparation for an even greater adventure. Our modern society has a different, more fearful view. To be old is to be ugly, and the character of life, written in the wrinkles and changes of the face and body, is seen as an expression of failure instead of completion. Instead of wisdom, there is senility; instead of the warm, loving clasp of family and friends, there is the emptiness of an old folks' home. Such a view holds little beauty.

There is a reality to our fear, but it is one that we have created for ourselves, based on the natural law of cause and effect. Aging is not the enemy, only the culmination of the habits of our life. If aging seems cruel, it is because we come to know too late the fate that we have created for ourselves.

Because we do not know the art of inner beauty, age becomes a terror. In response we have made a cult of youth, and we worship a superficial image. If there is emptiness, loneliness, and boredom, it is because we have failed to build the human bridges of family, friendship, and love. If there is fear, it is because we have failed to develop the one lasting value, that of spiritual understanding and fulfillment. And if there is ugliness, it is because we have failed to understand the true inner nature of beauty — physical, mental, and spiritual harmony and well-being.

We react to this fear and ugliness by more and more desperate attempts to create an image of youth. Our search for beauty becomes an expensive search for a superficial mask. A vast beauty industry has been built on the promise of a more youthful and beautiful image. And when the products can no longer hide the wrinkles and the sagging skin, we spend even more on cosmetic surgery. Even the sacred role of physician is subverted in our worship of a youthful image.

But these skin-deep changes that we so desperately buy are only that, a superficial mask that, at best, can only hide the reality of who we are for a brief time. Inevitably the mask becomes more fragile, more brittle as the underlying fear, disease, and the destructive habits of a lifetime come to their natural conclusion.

In buying the mask, by investing in the image, we cheat ourselves, not age. When we ignore our natural resources, a healthy body and mind, then whatever superficial changes we make are inherently self-defeating. The basis of our external beauty is our inner beauty, which is the expression of the inner harmony of body, mind, and spirit.

There is a far better way to achieve beauty. It lies in the potential of our body, mind, and spirit for harmony, balance, and health. It is the art of skillful living and graceful aging, the art and science of creating harmony within and without. This is the way of self-awareness, a technology of developing our inner natural resources, developing awareness and sensitivity to our environment, and using natural materials to enhance the expression of this inner harmony.

Rejuvenation is all about this way of beauty. It is a practical manual of knowledge and techniques that are so right, so timely, so profound in simplicity and truth, that it should, and will, shake an entire industry. *Rejuvenation* is more than a book on natural beauty, it is the thoughtful distillation of the experience of a master, a blending of ancient wisdom and modern knowledge.

The book begins with a discussion of harmony and balance. As a society, we rarely think in these terms, and when we do, it is often superficial, even trite. Yet nothing is more crucial to our health, our beauty and grace, and our personal fulfillment than inner harmony and balance.

We are really a citizen of two worlds — our inner mental world where we create the meaning of our life, and the outer world where we express and fulfill that meaning. Our body is the meeting ground of these two worlds. As the outer expression of who we are, the body and face are like a frozen picture of the mind. When we are unbalanced emotionally and physically, when we have disrupted and distorted our natural grace and inner harmony, we become dis-eased. This dis-ease is what we call stress, and it is the major cause of disease.

Ugliness is also the result of this dis-ease. When we have become unbalanced, when we are fearful, unloving, selfish, and mean-minded, no amount of skin cream can hide the bitter fruits of our disturbed mind. When our bodies are full of toxins, stuffed with unhealthy food and fat, and our blood pressure is too high, no surgeon can hide the consequences. And what cosmetics can hide the loneliness and depression that dims the light in our eyes? When internal harmony is distorted, our inner beauty and light is distorted, and our outer beauty becomes a mask, a caricature empty of any real value.

We also live in the external world. When we do not know how to live in harmony with those around us, we disturb our inner balance. When we form relationships that are unhealthy, dishonest, or unloving, we are out of harmony. When we eat foods that are unhealthy for us, we become unbalanced. When we breathe bad air, or use materials that are not a natural part of life, we become unbalanced. The concept of balance and harmony applies to all aspects of our life. If we are disturbed in one aspect, all other aspects will be affected. On the other hand, by bringing balance and harmony to one aspect of our life, all other aspects also benefit.

Beauty is an expression of who we are. When who we are is unbalanced, so is our beauty. But if we create harmony, within and without, then we will be beautiful. How we create that inner harmony and enhance the expression of that harmony is the real secret of beauty and graceful aging.

The chapters that follow compose an extraordinary manual on beauty and aging that is based on the natural harmony of body, mind, and spirit. The approach is necessarily holistic; that is, it involves all aspects of one's life, for beauty involves all aspects of one's life. The strength and power of this book is in its simplicity, practical techniques, and the knowledge gained from direct experience. It is a reflection of the author's personal study and knowledge. Horst knows his subject because he lives by the ideals and practices the techniques he presents.

I would like to add a personal note. I have known Horst for more than fifteen years. We have been, and are, brothers in a special tradition of meditation, life knowledge, and spiritual development. His devotion to knowledge and personal growth is both genuine and profound. Horst is not a dry academic. Rather, he is a visionary, an artist, and a scientist whose laboratory is his own life. His Aveda Corporation — manufacturer of pure and natural hair, skin, body care, and environmental products — is the expression of his knowledge and research. This book is truly a gift from one whose search for beauty is sincere, intense, and successful. I hold the utmost respect for this man Horst, and I know the reader of this book can only come to the same conclusion.

PHILLIP NUERNBERGER,   Ph.D.

❦ PREFACE

I HAVE WRITTEN THIS BOOK as one who is constantly
working to maintain the physical and mental balance. I taught
myself, and became aware through mentors, that we are solely
responsible for our own development. A part of our development is the constant search for perfection, and I now realize
that perfection already exists within and without. The true
lesson is to become aware of that existing perfection.

Rejuvenation is an expression of my work and life — to
restore the appearance and vigor of youth, which is to say the
physical and mental balance. Aging is much feared in our
culture because it is not understood, and because the elderly
command no respect. We need a new vision of aging that is
not the opposite of youth, but rather a process of growth that
can increase, instead of decrease, physical and mental vigor.

This book was written for those who are also seeking the
inner and outer balance, a way to age gracefully. I humbly
offer the fruits of my awareness, discoveries, and experiences
attained on my path of life.

H.R.

REJUVENATION

1 *HARMONY*

THIS BOOK IS DESIGNED as a practical guide to enhance beauty, health, and vitality and to help understand the aging process. Its principles can be applied to men and women of all ages and backgrounds. All of the exercises, formulas, physical and mental processes, and habit patterns described here are intended to create physical, mental, and spiritual balance. The "secret of youth" is achieving that state of equilibrium in which all levels of human functioning — physical, mental, spiritual — work in synergized harmony.

Cause and Effect

THE WAY TO REMAIN HEALTHY, youthful, and beautiful is to understand the law of cause and effect. Every mental and physical activity has its own cause, and each has its own effect. We alone are responsible for these effects. Today we have the information and, therefore, the opportunity to think and to act in a way that will keep us young throughout life.

If our activities create a sense of mental or physical imbalance, the effect will be a dis-ease within us. Continued over a long period of time, this imbalance can manifest itself in the form of disease. Surgery or medication at this time may temporarily correct the effect. However, if the causes of the dis-ease continue, remanifestation of those causes may occur sooner or later, in the same or different form.

Interaction with the environment and others can affect the way a person thinks and behaves. One person's behavior will affect other people's thoughts and behavior as well as their environment. This dynamic interactive process is continuous, and by being aware of our own thoughts and behavior, we can realize the potential consequences on others and the environment. On a broader level, everything in our environment can be seen as a manifestation of energy or movement, which begins on a sub-molecular level. All matter contains energy or *life force*. This vital life force, which is called *prana* or *chi* or *psi* energy, is all pervasive. It moves through and sustains all matter in the environment. Prana is responsible for coordinating all the interactions and the resulting consequences between all levels of existence within the environment. It is this invisible yet ever present life force that is the impetus and nourishment for all growth.

Yin and Yang

THE CONCEPT OF YIN AND YANG originates in the Chinese philosophy of Taoism. According to this philosophy all things are governed by a harmonious equilibrium, which is created through the unification of two contrary forces. Known as yin and yang, these two forces are components of prana, but prana is not typified by yin and yang characteristics. Through prana the yin and yang qualities are manifested. The contrary forces of yin and yang are characterized by the primordial states of feminine and masculine. All things in existence contain a particular individual balance between these two forces. Some of the yin and yang qualities are included in the following list:

Attribute	Yin	Yang
Tendency	Expansion	Contraction
Function	Diffusion	Fusion
Movement	More passive	More active
Vibration	High frequency	Low frequency

Attribute	Yin	Yang
Direction	Ascent	Descent
Position	Peripheral	Central
Weight	Lighter	Heavier
Temperature	Colder	Hotter
Light	Darker	Brighter
Humidity	Wetter	Drier
Density	Thinner	Thicker
Shape	Expansive	Contractive
Texture	Softer	Harder
Environment	Water	Earth
Sex	Female	Male
Attitude/ emotion	Passive	Aggressive
Work	Psychological	Physical
Mental function	Future oriented	Past oriented
Culture	Spiritual	Material
Dimension	Space	Time
Excitation	Sympathetic-nervous system	Parasympathetic-nervous system
Thought	Right brain	Left brain
Breath	Calm	Quick

Yin and yang existing in singular states represents imbalance; they are incomplete without each other. The unification of the two creates the complementary whole. It is not only possible to control these opposing forces, it is our responsibility to ourselves and others to learn and practice this science of equilibrium, which we discuss throughout this book. Only then can the true purpose of life be understood.

Youth Versus Aging

IN MODERN SOCIETY youth is admired while the elderly are often treated with disrespect. Few of us appreciate that old age is the culmination of a lifetime of experience, knowledge, and wisdom. Even though we know that aging is unavoidable, we have developed a subconscious fear of growing old. There are actually two fears involved. First is our fear of the unknown, or fear of the beyond. The second reason for subconsciously fearing old age is that we know how society treats the elderly and we are afraid that we, too, will be treated with disrespect. A vicious cycle begins because the fear of aging creates stress, and stress hastens the aging process. When we understand and practice the science of longevity, which is the balancing of one's physical and mental being, the fear of aging is replaced by constant awareness of the here and now. This balance is achieved by eating a balanced diet of healthy foods; nourishing the mind with positive thoughts and affirmations, while thoroughly organizing and digesting each thought; and choosing to live in a healthful environment.

Nourishment of the mind and body will be discussed at length in Chapter 4. At this point let us say that there are two types of food: *physiological food*, which is fed to and digested by the physical body, and *mental food,* which is fed to and digested by the psychological body. To be truly nourishing, physical and mental "foods" must contain the proper balance of positive and negative life forces.

The human body is radiantly healthy and, therefore, looks youthful and beautiful when the two opposite life-force energies — yin and yang — are in balance and harmony. For tissues to maintain integrity and to have the proper metabolism, this balanced state must exist on a subcellular level. Every part of the body is affected by the aging process. For example, dry, wrinkled skin indicates that the skin is gradually losing its ability to hold moisture and nourishment and that intra-cellular collagen, which is tissue cement, is not being properly restored. The body's inability to maintain collagen causes the skin to lose strength and elasticity. Smoking and emotional stress accelerate this degenerative process faster than any other known factors.

Remaining whole and healthy means eating wholesome, healthy foods that contain a proper, or harmonious, balance of nutrients for the body. For whole-body, or wholistic, health this harmonious state also must exist on the level of mental thoughts. For example, it is believed that separate activities occur in the left and right brain hemispheres. The right brain is thought to be the center for creative thinking, or the feminine aspect of human personality; the left brain the center for logical thinking, or the counterpart masculine personality. These two thinking processes complement each other. If there is no balance or integration between our ability to think creatively and to think logically, disorder in thinking processes will occur.

Much has been written in modern psychology about mental integration and positive thinking as a means for remaining young and healthy. But these ideas are not new. The great masters have always taught that youth is not primarily a state of the body but, rather, a state of mind. A youthful thought is one which is affirming, positive, and spiritual or prayerful. This type of thought helps us learn from, rather than dwell in, the past. Aging results from years of destructive thinking, self-reproach, and blaming others. By contrast, youthful thoughts keep us in touch with reality and give us reason to live.

We can begin to see that we have a great deal of influence over aging, and even more over the quality of the aging process. We will all age, but this should be a process of fulfillment and growth, not a process of degeneration, disease, and helplessness. By understanding ourselves — our physical, mental, and spiritual needs — and through the daily practice of thinking, eating, and breathing correctly one will begin to see that today's activities have certain effects tomorrow. By knowing the tools and techniques to properly serve these needs, the aging process will bring the joy, wisdom, and contentment that is the natural fulfillment of our life.

2 *THE SCIENCE OF LONGEVITY*

Ayurveda

Ayurveda IS A SANSKRIT TERM that means the science of longevity. The Ayurvedic system is a wholistic approach to maintaining and regaining health, and it has been practiced in India for over five thousand years. It is a science of daily living that includes a vast library of knowledge on physical exercise, nutrition, herbology and pharmacology, massage, and even surgery, psychiatry, and meditation.

Ayurvedic techniques are designed to establish and maintain balance in the body and mind, and, therefore, prevent dis-ease and prolong healthy life. Practitioners of Ayurveda assess the conditions of the individual as a whole and match their recommendations to each individual's unique constitution and temperament. In Ayurveda there are three basic constitutional elements, or *doshas,* which govern all of the human physiological and psychological functions. The doshas are 1) *kapha,* or all that is heavy, dense, and material (earth-like); 2) *pitta,* or that which is energetic and assertive (fire-like); and 3) *vata,* the most subtle and active and the least tangible elements (wind-like). Each individual is born with a particular combination of elements and a predominant tendency toward one or more. However, this combination varies in response to the constantly changing interaction between our internal and external environments. Through the science of Ayurveda, internal balance is created in the body and mind by changing our diet and lifestyle habits. As an example of a dietary change, a person with a predominantly kapha constitution who is overweight may feel more active and energetic if he or she eats foods that are slightly more pungent (pitta) or bitter (vata). In Ayurveda, food, spices, and herbs are natural remedies that are used as part of a daily routine to balance our physical and psychological systems. Similarly, special exercises and breathing techniques also may be recommended to restore balance and to prevent dis-ease and the debilitating effects of premature aging.

The Ayurvedic system is complex and many years of intensive training and experience are needed to understand it. However, a growing number of physicians today now incorporate the principles of Ayurveda into their lives and their medical practices. Their approach to the prevention of disease combines the technology of modern medicine with proper nutrition, physical exercise, and natural herbal remedies. These are the physicians who will play a major role in helping us to extend the human lifespan and usher in a new age of wellness.

External Hygiene
SYNTHETIC CHEMICALS VERSUS NATURAL PRODUCTS

The lack of hygiene has always been a major factor in the cause and spread of disease and, consequently, in shortening the human lifespan. The spread of bacterial growth, which leads to infection, is now controlled chemically, but this technological advance has created new problems. Manufacturers of chemical agents to control bacteria use mostly synthetic substances in their products, which are produced on a mass scale for worldwide markets. Synthetic chemicals are also found in nearly all the commercial products we use, from fertilizers and insect repellents to disinfectants and soaps for household use and cleansers and deodorants for the body. We ingest harmful chemicals like DDT in the food we eat, and we inhale vast quantities of carbon monoxide and other pollutants in the air we breathe. Similar chemicals, equally powerful but with no harmful side effects, are found in nature. But because they are more costly, requiring more time and skill to extract, they are a commercially unacceptable alternative to profit-oriented producers.

ENVIRONMENTAL BALANCING

It is not just our bodies that are being polluted with synthetic chemicals but mother nature as well. We have created a toxic environment and the effects are tragic — dying forests, polluted and stagnant bodies of water, reduced fish populations, the extinction of some species of wildlife, and the development of new diseases as a result of chemical poisoning. Few people realize the magnitude of our environmental problems. Famine and environmental disorder have become the norm despite the fact that we have more technological expertise than ever before. Ecological collapse is occurring in large and small ways throughout the world because humankind no longer practices environmental balancing. If manufacturers would choose to use nature's ingredients in their products, the producers and suppliers of raw materials would be encouraged to farm more naturally; this planet could again be the beautiful garden it once was, and all living species could be preserved.

The principles of environmental health and balance are much the same for the external world and our internal world. As we grow older we observe certain conditions developing, such as rheumatism, arthritis, cellulite deposits, cholesterol build up, and stretch marks. These effects, which we call aging, are caused by insufficient lubrication of the body's tissues. Essential oils in the body are not replenished because we are not cleansing and nourishing our systems properly. Earth, too, can be envisioned as a body. The same pollutants that cause us to age are also affecting the body of our planet. The symptoms of age and decay on earth are similar to the body's aging symptoms. For example, the "skin," or outer layer of the earth, is beginning to dry and crack as we extract minerals and nutrients from the earth's surface without replenishing them.

Our failure to replace these nutrients is having catastrophic effects. This environmental dilemma is caused by our neglect and disrespect for the planet. The dictionary defines "worship" as the act of showing respect, honor, and courtesy. At a deeper level, our failure to care for the environment is tantamount to refusing to worship nature, which is a manifestation of the Divine, by showing the proper respect. The best way to develop sensitivity to the needs of the earth's body is, first, to become aware of the needs of our own bodies.

Aromatherapy

THROUGHOUT THIS BOOK, we discuss the properties of yin and yang as they occur in the mineral, plant, and animal kingdoms. Everything in the Universe is a manifestation of these two opposite energies or forces, which attract and balance each other. If one or the other force is predominant, imbalance and disharmony can occur. It is essential to maintain a balance of these energies in the body and mind. Yet, opposition can be used to balance out an extreme condition. For example, if a condition exists that is hot or stimulated (yang), cooling or calming (yin) properties may be used to balance the condition. This balancing practice, through use of opposites, can also apply to balancing ourselves psychologically. Each plant and flower essence is dominant in either one or the other extremes of yin and yang, as are the psychological conditions of the mind. Once the message of the essence has been communicated to the brain through the olfactory system, a reaction is stimulated by way of the sympathetic and parasympathetic nervous systems and there is a corresponding psychological reaction. The messages may have either a stimulating or calming effect on a variety of conditions, and in many cases it can have both effects, leaving one alert and calm, thus balancing an existing extreme.

Flowers and herbs are especially pure and potent sources of yin-yang energies. A plant in full bloom is at the peak of its growth, and the life force (prana or chi) in a flowering plant is in its most active and potent state. Each plant's life force is a unique combination of properties known as the absolute essense. The absolute essense gives flowers and plants their individual aromas, and different aromas have different effects on us psychologically and physiologically. In their purest state, these essences function as natural remedies, because they re-establish mental and physical balance.

The absolute essence is present in the plant in the form of invisible molecular gases. In aromatherapy, plants are harvested in full bloom and put through a special distillation process. Through evaporation and distillation the absolute essence of the plant is extracted in a liquid form, and the natural properties are obtained at their highest level of purity and potency. In this way the plant's life force lives on in potent form even after its flowers have died. Any substance that is pure and potent will be extremely active on the gaseous level or as the molecules disperse. This is why natural essences have such a revitalizing effect. We can feel and even see the physical and mental energy that comes from these pure, potent natural sources. What we are actually seeing and feeling is the vital life force, released in its purest form.

Aromatherapy and aromaology are based upon the principles of Ayurveda — found in ancient scriptures of the Far East. Aromaology is the study of aromas and aromatherapy is the application of that knowledge. The Egyptians, who were among the earliest practitioners of aromatherapy, vaporized floral and herbal oils in small pots of boiling water to soften the skin, soothe the mind, and normalize the functions of various glands. Ayurvedic medical texts even specify which oils to use for which glands. The Aztecs had special vapor-bath rooms called *temezcals*, which were similar to the Finnish sauna. Hot, dry air in the room was filled with the vapors of flowers and herb oils rising from a small pool of stones and hot water. These vapors were thought to stimulate circulation, soften the skin, and contribute to a relaxed frame of mind.

USES FOR ESSENTIAL OILS The use of essential oils for the treatment of physical imbalances is a healthy and safe alternative to many synthetic treatments. These oils, however, are not to be considered a substitute for the supervision of a medical doctor. When buying essential oils, be certain that there is a written guarantee that the oils are pharmaceutically pure.

When applying an essential oil to a skin condition, combine the oil(s) with a base oil. Pure evening primrose oil is an exceptional base, as is jojoba oil or any high quality clarified plant oil.

When working with an internal condition, combine the essence or essences with warm distilled water and a teaspoon of honey or brown sugar.

BLOOD, HEART, AND CIRCULATION CONDITIONS

Anemia — camomile, garlic, lemon, thyme

Chest pains — aniseed, basil, caraway, neroli

Chills — cinnamon, clove, melissa, rosemary, ru-khus, thyme

Circulation problems — cypress, garlic, lemon, melissa, rosemary, ru-khus, thyme

Lazy heart — aniseed, borneo camphor, cayenne pepper, garlic

Low energy — basil, cinnamon, clove, garlic, geranium, hyssop, marjoram, nutmeg, pine

DIGESTIVE CONDITIONS

Colic — aniseed, basil, bergamot, hyssop, motti, peppermint

Constipation — camomile, cardamom, geranium, lavender, rose, terebinth, ylang-ylang

Diarrhea — cinnamon, clove, garlic, ginger, juniper, lemon, neroli, nutmeg, peppermint, sage, sandalwood

Indigestion — aniseed, basil, bergamot, camomile, cinnamon, clove, fennel, garlic, lavender, nutmeg, peppermint, thyme

Intestinal gas — aniseed, basil, bergamot, camomile, caraway, cinnamon, clove, coriander, eucalyptus, fennel, garlic, geranium, ginger, hyssop, lemon, marjoram, nutmeg, peppermint, rose, rosemary, sage, savory, tarragon, thyme

Intestinal inflammation — camomile, eucalyptus, geranium, rose, ylang-ylang

Intestinal spasms — aniseed, bergamot, cajeput, camomile, cinnamon, clove, eucalyptus, fennel, garlic, geranium, lavender, peppermint, pine, rose, savory, tarragon, terebinth

Intestinal ulcers — camomile, geranium, jasmine, lemon, neroli, rose, vanilla, ylang-ylang

MALE AND FEMALE
CONDITIONS

Bladder infection — clary sage, hyssop, marjoram

Breast congestion — aniseed, black pepper, cajeput, eucalyptus, fennel, fir, garlic, geranium, hyssop, juniper, lavender, lemon, niaouli, peppermint, pine, rosemary, sage, thyme, ylang-ylang

Cold sores/herpes — cajeput, camomile, coriander, geranium, lemon, peppermint, rosemary

Enlarged prostate — neroli, rose, thuja

Genital/urinary infection — cajeput, camomile, coriander, hyssop, juniper, lavender, niaouli, thyme, ylang-ylang

Impotence — aniseed, cinnamon, clover, frankincense, genet, ginger, juniper, melissa, myrrh, patchouli, peppermint, pine, sandalwood, thyme, vanilla, ylang-ylang

Lactation (to increase) — aniseed, caraway, fennel, lemongrass, rose, ylang-ylang

Lactation (to reduce) — jasmine, peppermint, sage

Menopause — all oils

Menstrual cramps — aniseed, cajeput, camomile, clary sage, cypress, eucalyptus, juniper, marjoram, peppermint, rose, rosemary, tarragon, ylang-ylang

Menstruation (to promote) — cajeput, camomile, cypress, hyssop, origanum, peppermint, sage, thyme

MENTAL/EMOTIONAL
WELLNESS

Anxiety — basil, camomile, eucalyptus, jasmine, marjoram, motti, neroli, rose, thyme, ylang-ylang

Depression — borneo camphor, camomile, jasmine, lavender, motti, nutmeg, thyme, verbena

Dizziness/fainting — cinnamon, nutmeg, peppermint, rosemary, wintergreen

Headache — camomile, cardamom, lavender, lemon, motti, peppermint, rosemary, wintergreen

Hypertension — balsam, camomile, foin, garlic, genet, jasmine, lavender, lemon, lotus, marjoram, motti, pine, rose, rosemary, valinium, vanilla, ylang-ylang

Hysteria — cajeput, camomile, jasmine, lavender, motti, neroli, nutmeg, peppermint, rose, rosemary

Irritability — camomile, cypress, jasmine, lavender, marjoram, melissa, motti, nutmeg, rose, vanilla, verbena

Migraine — aniseed, basil, camomile, eucalyptus, lavender, lemon, marjoram, motti, peppermint, rose, rosemary, sesame, terebinth, vanilla, verbena

Nerves (general tonic) — camomile, cinnamon, cypress, frankincense, genet, jasmine, lavender, marjoram, motti, neroli, nutmeg, orange, rose, sage, sandalwood, verbena

Stress/fatigue — basil, camomile, cinnamon, clove, cypress, frankincense, genet, jasmine, lavender, marjoram, motti, neroli, orange, rose, sage, savory, sandalwood, thyme, vanilla

PERSONAL AND HOME HYGIENE

Body deodorizer — cypress, frankincense, jasmine, lavender, rose, sandalwood, vanilla

Household disinfectant — aniseed, cajeput, eucalyptus, hyssop, juniper, lemon, orange, pine, rosemary, sage, wintergreen

RESPIRATORY CONDITIONS

Asthma — aniseed, cajeput, cardamom, eucalyptus, fir, garlic, hyssop, juniper, lavender, lemon, marjoram, niaouli, origanum, peppermint, pine, rosemary, sage, savory, thyme

Bronchitis — cajeput, cardamom, eucalyptus, fir, garlic, hyssop, juniper, lavender, lemon, niaouli, origanum, peppermint, pine, rosemary, sage, sandalwood, savory, terebinth, thyme

Cough — aniseed, eucalyptus, fennel, geranium, neroli, rose

SKIN DISORDERS

Acne/boils — bergamot, cajeput, cedarwood, cypress, ginger, juniper, lavender, myrrh, sandalwood

Athlete's foot — eucalyptus, fir, juniper, lavender, lemon, pine, rosemary, wintergreen

Chapped skin — jojoba, rose, sandalwood, ylang-ylang

Cuts — cajeput, camomile, coriander, eucalyptus, hyssop, lavender, peppermint, rosemary, sage, thyme

Eczema — cajeput, camomile, eucalyptus, geranium, hyssop, jasmine, neroli, pennywort, rose, sage, turmeric

Insect bites — basil, cinnamon, garlic, lavender, lemon, sage, savory, thyme. *Insect repellent* — cajeput, clove, eucalyptus, geranium, ginger lily, lavender, peppermint, sage

Itching — camomile, eucalyptus, geranium, neroli, rose

Psoriasis — cajeput, camomile, eucalyptus, neroli, sandalwood

Rash — camomile, eucalyptus, rose, sandalwood, ylang-ylang

Sensitive skin — camomile, frankincense, geranium, lavender, rose, ylang-ylang

Skin rejuvenation — cinnamon, eucalyptus, fennel, garlic, genet, jasmine, juniper, lotus, melissa, neroli, niaouli, pine, rose, rosemary, sandalwood, thyme, violet, ylang-ylang

Sunburn — camomile, eucalyptus, geranium, lavender, rose, sesame, ylang-ylang

STOMACH CONDITIONS   *Gastritis* — lemon

Loss of appetite — basil, bergamot, camomile, caraway, coriander, fennel, garlic, ginger, hyssop, juniper, lemon, nutmeg, sage, tarragon

Nervous indigestion — aniseed, camomile, caraway, coriander, eucalyptus, geranium, neroli, rose, savory, tarragon

Nervous vomiting — aniseed, cajeput, camomile, eucalyptus, fennel, geranium, peppermint, rose, ylang-ylang

Stomach pains — basil, cinnamon, fennel, geranium, hyssop, peppermint, pine, rose, rosemary, tarragon

Stomach ulcer — camomile, coriander, eucalyptus, geranium, lemon, neroli, rose

OTHER CONDITIONS   *Earache* — camomile, sandalwood

Sore muscles — eucalyptus, frankincense, geranium, lavender, lemon, melissa, myrrh, peppermint, wintergreen

Sore throat — aniseed, basil, clove, coriander, eucalyptus, fennel, peppermint

THE MEDICAL APPLICATIONS OF AROMATHERAPY   Private research in the science of aromatherapy has been going on for years. This research includes gathering facts and materials from around the world, researching ancient texts, and recording the experiences and reactions in the use of pure distilled essences. Because of this research and subsequent developments in the field, new and healthy alternatives are now being offered to the general public.

The therapeutic potential of aromatherapy is being studied optimistically by the medical field. Medical doctors are beginning to agree that essential oils may serve as effective remedies in behavioral problems. The main thrust of current medical research compares the effects of natural and synthetic aromas on a variety of symptoms. These effects are monitored by observing the changes in a variety of autonomic responses — body temperature, muscle tension, perspiration, pulse rate, and brain waves.

By learning how natural aromas can be used to calm, stimulate, and regulate the human body, a new approach to treating illness can be developed, freeing people from reliance on synthetics that frequently have negative side effects. It is encouraging to see the response of medical professionals and their motivation to expand research in this fascinating field.

THE SENSE OF SMELL

The sense of smell protects us from harmful or unhygienic conditions and alerts us to contaminated or spoiled foods, pollutants, and other toxins in our environment. Smell helps us identify and classify the thousands of elements in the world around us. Yet it relates not only to how we interpret our surroundings, but also to our memory and emotions.

The relationship between smell, memory, and emotions is physical. Aromas are actually molecules floating in the air. As we encounter them, a chain reaction of physical responses occurs within our brain and body. For example, the smell of smoke may cause us to sneeze, or the aroma of baking cookies might make our mouth water. But beyond the physical reaction, the aroma of baking cookies may also recall pleasant memories of a warm kitchen from our childhood, just as a medicinal smell may conjure up memories of a visit to the doctor, and in turn the fear, anxiety, and pain we felt there.

This phenomenon of recalling emotions and memories associated with a smell is called *memory response.* The term simply means that when we have an experience that is associated with a particular smell both the experience and the smell will be recorded in memory. Later in life, when we re-encounter the smell again, it will remind us of that experience and the emotions related to that experience.

There are three steps to the body's assimilation of smells: reception, transmission, and perception.

1. Reception — Aroma molecules are inhaled up through the nasal passages where they encounter and bind to the olfactory epithelium (receptor) cells.

2. Transmission — As the molecule binds to the receptor cell, a message is fired to the olfactory bulbs located at the base of the brain. At this point, a variety of cells (glomeruli, mitral cells, and granule neurons) assist in interpreting and giving feedback on the aroma message.

    The mitral neurons transmit this message to the limbic system, which is the area of the brain that deals with memory and emotion. It is in the limbic lobe where all the senses, including smell, are synergized. And it is the limbic system that activates the hypothalamus.

3. Perception — The hypothalamus is the controller for the pituitary gland, tying smell messages directly to the internal chemistry of the body.

    The pituitary, on cue from the hypothalamus, releases chemical messages into the bloodstream, activating hormones and regulating body functions.

FIGURE 2.1:   The olfactory system

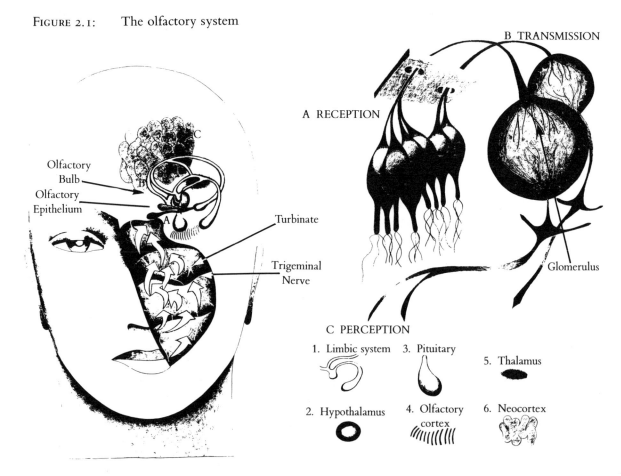

16

The olfactory cortex helps in distinguishing different odors. This is also the area where perception of synthetic versus natural will occur.

The thalamus is the connector of aroma messages of the limbic system to the higher function of the neocortex.

Unfortunately, our olfactory system becomes desensitized from daily exposure to synthetic fragrances, flavors, and toxins. As we grow older it becomes more and more difficult to distinguish one aroma from another.

There are two ways to retune and refine this sense — one is by adopting a lifestyle of wholistic (whole body) health including proper diet, physical activity, breathing, and mental exercises; the other is by using pure, unalloyed cosmetics and household products that will develop our sensitivity to healthy, natural fragrances.

Aromatherapy products, made from the pure essences of plants and flowers, are specially suited for retraining the senses. Unlike natural aromas, synthetic aromas are manufactured in laboratories with gasoline by-products. These artificial fragrances do not carry nature's organic molecular structure, nor the therapeutic benefits of natural aromas.

COSMETICS AND HOUSEHOLD PRODUCTS

Some of history's most beautiful and successful women and men are known to have followed beauty regimens using compounds of herbs and flowers with such good results that their recipes have become legendary. With the advent of ready-made cosmetics, many fashionable, urban women stopped using those regimens. But in some areas of the world, such as China and India, herbal and floral cosmetic and medicinal preparations never fell into disuse. In much of the East and in several European peasant cultures the ancient knowledge of aromatherapy has been preserved and further developed. Modern researchers are now turning to these sources to begin their inquiries into the science of aromatherapy.

The future of the cosmetics industry may one day involve widespread use of aromatherapy as an important method of balancing and harmonizing the body and mind. Many companies who once disregarded and even ridiculed this science are now beginning to apply the concepts to their own products and in some cases have slowly begun to do their own research. Thus the cosmetic industry is stepping into a new dimension of personal care products that will benefit the body as well as the mind. Similarly, household products made from absolute essences will help control bacterial growth and restore life and balance to our polluted, deteriorating planet.

NATURAL INGREDIENTS   The cosmetics and household products we use every day should come from natural sources. This is because substances found in nature can 1) nourish and cleanse without polluting our systems and 2) be safely returned to earth once we have used them. Even today there are many essences of flowers, herbs, barks, roots, and other natural "whole foods" that are being used effectively in cosmetics and household products. Some of these pure, natural ingredients and their benefits are listed below. Look for them and their benefits when choosing products.

Aloe — A natural emollient and moisturizer, aloe is often used to soothe minor burns. It absorbs into the hair and scalp, making the hair more manageable, and it helps soothe a dry, itchy scalp.

Anise — A derivitive of aniseed, anise is an antispasmodic that works primarily on the digestive system. Anise also works as a general stimulant on the cardiac, respiratory, and digestive systems. Specifically, anise may be used for colic in infants, nausea, gas, and pain due to overeating.

Arnica — Arnica has a long history of use as a natural remedy in the Ayurvedic systems. It is an excellent emollient and also soothes skin disorders and breakouts, acting somewhat like an antibiotic. Arnica helps reduce swelling and has a stimulating effect on the circulatory system.

Bakul — Bakul is an East Indian oil, and its essences are taken from the flower and the roots of the bakul plant. Bakul refreshes the skin and also serves as a moisturizer.

Basil — The word basil derives from the Greek word *basilicon* and means royal ointment or remedy. Basil has both cooling and warming properties, and is beneficial for use on sluggish, congested skin, or as a general tonic/refresher. It is also good for fainting, bronchitis, depression, gout, insomnia, migraine, nausea, vomiting, giving the mind clarity and relieving intellectual fatigue. The action of basil is enhanced when it is used with other essences.

Benzoin resinoid — Derived from a gum taken from a variety of trees, it is extremely useful in cases of respiratory distress, such as asthma and bronchitis. Benzoin resinoid is effective in reducing skin irritations, redness, and itching.

Bergamot — Bergamot oil comes from the extracted essence of the rind of a fruit from the bergamot tree. It is one of the principal ingredients in classical eau de colognes. It makes a very pleasant, refreshing, and relaxing bath oil. It moisturizes and also helps soften calloused skin.

Black pepper — This common spice stimulates circulation, helping in the elimination of toxins. It also has heating properties and is good for colds, constipation, fever, loss of appetite, and vomiting.

Borneol (borneo camphor) — Derived from a tree in Sumatra, it works as a powerful antiseptic and also functions as a cardiac tonic. This substance is believed to stimulate the adrenal cortex.

Cajeput — Soothing for tired, overworked muscles, cajeput stimulates local circulation and calms irritations.

Camomile — Camomile is an herb with a wonderful aroma. It helps maintain healthy tissues and cleanses pores of impurities.

Camphor — This useful essence is an ideal remedy to apply before and after exercise. It has the dual effect of cooling and heating, and it stimulates the skin and the circulation.

Caraway — Commonly used as a condiment in sauces, breads, and meats, caraway is an excellent digestive stimulant and diuretic, as well as being helpful in reducing intestinal gas.

Cedarwood — This ancient essence was highly valued by the Egyptians for use in cosmetics and in the preservation of mummies. Cedarwood is beneficial for use on all kinds of skin eruptions; its action is astringent and soothing.

Cinnamon — Cinnamon has definite warming qualities and thus is effective for aches from colds and fevers. It is useful in cases of breathing difficulties, fainting, sluggish digestion, and toothaches.

Clary sage — An astringent that tones tissue and works as an excellent nerve tonic, clary sage is also good for boils, depression, gas, and skin care.

Clove — Clove is an antiseptic that helps maintain healthy tissue and cleanses pores of impurities.

Comfrey — This most valuable herb helps promote the formation of new cells. Comfrey contains allantoin, a healing agent extracted from the comfrey root. It has soothing emollient properties and due to its softening properties, it is also useful in moisturizing and sunburn lotions, in ointments, and in massage and body oils. Comfrey has properties that soothe skin disorders and breakouts, and it is slightly astringent in nature.

Coriander — Often associated with apertifs and liqueurs, it is used mainly for digestion and the stimulation of appetite. Coriander is an excellent stomach tonic and also contributes to strengthening the heart and expelling gas from the bowels.

Cypress — Cypress is a powerful astringent that helps stay abnormal, irregular, or excessive skin discharges.

Echinacea — Echinacea is the strong smelling root of a wild growing plant. It acts as an astringent and has been used throughout history to prevent skin disorders and imbalances.

Essence d'armiose — Extracted from a shrub grown in the Himalayan foothills, this oil has a powerful fresh, bittersweet aroma with a gentle cooling effect. It works very well as a gargle and may also be used in soaps.

Eucalyptus — This natural essence was regarded as a general all-purpose remedy in the latter part of the nineteenth century. It has a soothing and cooling effect on skin and acts as a mild stimulant, which helps increase blood circulation. Eucalyptus has been used to soothe blisters, burns, and scalds.

Fennel — Fennel is commonly found in Europe and along the shore of the Mediterranean. It was well known to the ancient Greeks and was cultivated by the Romans. Fennel is a good internal cleanser because it helps rid the organs and blood of impurities. This, in turn, helps reduce wrinkles caused by dryness and corrects bad color in the skin.

Flax seed — This herbal extract is often used as a hair conditioner and emollient, and it builds body in the hair. Its soothing effects also help balance skin disorders.

Frankincense — Frankincense has been widely used in skin care preparations for centuries and was one of the most highly prized substances of the ancient world. It was used first as incense and later in cosmetics and toiletries. Ovid, the Roman poet, recommends frankincense as an excellent preparation for toilet purposes. Frankincense is an activator that warms and soothes the skin, and it also has astringent qualities; its aroma helps to calm the nervous system.

Garlic — Garlic is effective for digestive disorders such as sluggish digestion and diarrhea and also works for colds and other lung problems. Use garlic for warts, corns and calluses, as well as infected sores.

Geranium — This delightfully sweet, fresh scent is a refreshing astringent and a mild skin tonic. It is useful in soothing skin disorders. Like camphor it has a dual heating/cooling effect on the skin.

Ginger — The therapeutic benefits of ginger are varied but focus mainly in the digestive area. It helps to relieve painful digestion and also works to stimulate the appetite. Use ginger to treat a sore throat.

Jasmine — The jasmine plant is a creeper with white or yellow flowers. It is cultivated in Algeria, Morocco, France, China, Egypt, Italy, and Turkey. Jasmine is one of the most exquisite of scents; it is also one of the most expensive essences and is used in many of the costliest perfumes. The name is derived from the Arabic *yasmin*. In China, the flowers are used in cosmetics, and an infused oil was used in former times to massage the body after bathing. This essential oil cools skin redness and itching and conditions the skin. Jasmine works on both a physical and emotional level and is of great value in promoting positive feelings and confidence. It is most useful for removing apathy, indifference, or listlessness. Throughout history, jasmine has also been known as an aphrodisiac.

Jojoba oil — The edible seeds of the jojoba plant are known to contain the oil most closely resembling our bodies' natural protective, youth-giving oil, sebum. Jojoba nourishes and rejuvenates the hair and skin (or scalp). It also serves as a stabilizer, and it restores moisture balance.

Juniper — Distilled from juniper berries, juniper promotes sweating to release toxins. It also works as an astringent and tissue toner.

Lavender — The word lavender comes from the Latin word *lavare*, meaning "to wash." It was one of the favorite aromas of the Romans and was used in their bathing activities. Lavender is generally regarded as one of the most useful and versatile essences for therapeutic purposes. Its properties are a fairly equal balance between yin and yang properties and, therefore, it is considered neutral. Lavender has a calming, soothing effect on inflammations, and it helps rejuvenate skin cells and prevent sunburn. It also calms breakouts and skin disorders and has been used as a deodorant. Lavender is known for its great hair conditioning properties.

Lemon — This essence, which comes from the outer layer of the rind, can be effective in cases of gout, arthritis, and scurvy. Lemon is good for cleansing water and also helps to stimulate the appetite.

Lemongrass — This is a perennial grass with similar qualities to lemon. It is effective in stimulating sluggish digestion and is also recognized for increasing human milk production.

Marjoram — This herb was widely used by the Greeks in medicine, perfumes, and toiletries. There is a special comforting effect associated with marjoram. It makes a relaxing, warming, fortifying bath oil and is an excellent cleanser. Its sedative and warming qualities make it an effective body massage oil for overworked muscles.

Melissa — Referred to as the "Elixir of Life," melissa seems to have the wonderful ability of uplifting one's spirits. Its qualities are both calming and sedating, making it a superb relaxant and antispasmodic. Melissa smells much like lemon with an herbal undertone and is said to be an effective healing agent for both the mind and the emotions.

Menthol — This aromatic substance is the active portion of peppermint oil and is well known for its cooling, refreshing effect. It relieves skin irritations and provides a cooling effect as a skin tonic.

Myrrh — Gum myrrh (from which the oil is extracted) exudes from branches of the myrrh shrub, which grows in northeast Africa in very dry conditions, and is most commonly found in southern Arabia. It is also found in the "Garden of Eden," the land between the rivers Tigris and Euphrates, which was part of Babylonia in the time of Moses. Myrrh was probably more widely used than any other aromatic in ancient times for incense, perfumes, and medicines. At Heliopolis, the ancient Egyptians used to burn myrrh at noon every day as part of their sun-worshipping ritual. It has been used by many people in many ways for at least three thousand years and is still a very popular remedy. Myrrh helps to cool, moisturize, and rejuvenate the skin, and it balances skin disorders.

Neroli oil — Oil of orange blossoms, known as neroli oil, is extracted from the white blossoms of the bitter orange. The orange tree is a native of China where the flowers have been used for centuries in cosmetic preparations. It is now cultivated in France, Tunisia, Italy, and the United States. Neroli oil is among the finest of flower essences. It is calming for irritation and redness and soothing for dry skin and broken veins.

Niaouli — This is a rather intense essence that is useful for lung problems, such as bronchitis and asthma. Niaouli can also be helpful in cases of intestinal parasites.

Nutmeg — Nutmeg is a mild substance that is helpful in cases of digestive problems and intestinal infections. It has also been used as an aid for toothaches, scanty menstrual cycles, and for eliminating bad breath.

Onion — Among Bulgarians (great onion eaters), many centenarians may be counted. The onion has been recognized as being helpful for growing pains, stress, stings, boils, burns, warts, and corns.

Patchouli — Derived from a patchouli plant, this oil helps eliminate excess tissue fluid and is good for anxiety, depression, skin care, and wounds.

Pennyroyal — A species of mint found most commonly near marshes and streams, this potent essence is very warming and promotes perspiration. It is useful in cases of toothaches and headaches and helps clear skin of bruises and blemishes. Pennyroyal is helpful in regulating the menstrual cycle, but due to its potent nature it should be avoided by pregnant women.

Peppermint — This is one of the most important therapeutic oils. It was used for centuries by Greek, Roman, and Egyptian physicians. Peppermint relieves skin irritations while providing a cooling effect as a skin tonic. It is an invigorating and refreshing bath oil that helps cool the body, especially in the summer.

Petitgrain oil — Petitgrain oil is distilled from the leaves and young shoots of the bitter orange tree. This is the same tree from which neroli is obtained. While several varieties of petitgrain are available, the largest amounts are produced in Paraguay, where only cultivated trees are used in the production of the oil. Petitgrain has an astringent effect, and it tones tissues and helps balance skin disorders.

Pine — This is a potent essence that is effective in cases of respiratory and urinary infections, intestinal pains, gout, gallstones, and lice.

Rose — Roses have been used from time immemorial for their appearance, their scent, and their therapeutic properties. Rose oil was first used in Persia. Today the finest rose oil comes from Bulgaria (from the damask rose). It takes sixty thousand roses (about one hundred eighty pounds) to make one ounce of rose oil! Rose oil soothes nervous tension, cools inflamed skin, tones capillaries, reduces redness and has a mild astringent effect.

Rosemary — The name, rosemary, comes from the Latin *rose marinus* meaning sea dew, as it is fond of water. One of the earliest, most renowned English medicinal herbs, rosemary water was used as a beautifying and cleansing facial wash. Rosemary has a warming, stimulating effect on the skin and increases local circulation. It has been used to help baldness, burns, headaches, hypertension, and rheumatism. It is also a nourishing, astringent skin tonic and an excellent hair conditioner that makes the hair lustrous.

Sage — Sage is an extremely versatile essence with a multitude of uses. It helps speed the healing of wounds, works as an expectorant in the respiratory system, and makes a superb general tonic. Sage is also effective in cases of sore throat and headaches and is said to stimulate the memory.

Sandalwood — Sandalwood has been used from earliest times. It is mentioned in the Nirukta, the oldest known Vedic commentary, which was written during the fifth century B.C. In India and Egypt it was used as a perfume and was an ingredient in many cosmetics. Sandalwood has been used medicinally and in expensive perfumes. It is one of the most useful oils for the skin, soothing itchy, overworked skin and acting as an analgesic, antiseptic, moisturizer, and emollient; it also helps moisturize tissues for oily skin. Sandalwood also has a calming effect on the mind.

Sarsaparilla — Sarsaparilla is a natural skin nourisher, which promotes sweating to release toxins. In this way it soothes itchy, broken, or irritated skin and helps reduce spots and bad odors emanating from the skin.

Siberian fir — This essence stimulates circulation and helps in the elimination of accumulated waste products.

Slippery elm — The inner bark is very gelatinous and contains protein. When mixed with other substances it helps them adhere to the skin surface. High in natural nutrients, it is sometimes used in a soothing poultice (skin pack) application for skin disorders and breakouts. It is also a common ingredient in lozenges for coughs and sore throats.

Spearmint — Spearmint is an effective agent for a variety of stomach disorders as well as a calmitive for the nerves; it is good for colic, gas in the stomach and bowels, as well as vomiting due to pregnancy. Spearmint should not be boiled.

Tarragon — Although a well-known herb used in cooking, tarragon also has a variety of therapeutic qualities. It is helpful in cases of sluggish digestion, loss of appetite, and hiccoughs. It has also been recommended for painful menstruation.

Terebinth — Terebinth is considered helpful in cases of urinal and renal infections.

Thyme — Recognized as an effective aid for the mind and the nerves, thyme is suggested in cases of anxiety, depression, insomnia, and fatigue. Thyme may also be used for bites, boils, sores, and stings.

Wintergreen — This potent essence, obtained from an American herb of the same name, gives a warming, stimulating effect to the skin and increases local circulation. It helps to prepare the body for physical activity and, afterwards, it helps the body return to its normal balance.

White oak bark — White oak bark is an astringent and helps the skin resist infection. It has been known to reduce heat and scabs and arrest irregular, excessive, or abnormal discharges.

Ylang-ylang — This is one of the most pleasant oils and may be used as a perfume or exotic bath oil. It calms the nervous system, acting as a sedative to counteract anxiety and tension, and soothes the skin.

Some of the essences from flowers and herbs listed above can be toxic when used in highly concentrated form.[2] For example, wintergreen is one of the main ingredients in deep-heating ointments, and when diluted it is also a strong and effective household cleanser. However, in its pure and undiluted state, it is extremely hot and can sting the skin. We recommend that oils in their pure state be kept out of the reach of children and that direct contact with the skin and eyes be avoided.

Essential oils should make up no more than two to three percent of a product's entire list of ingredients. Small amounts of essential oils can be combined effectively with a natural detergent or with some other oils such as jojoba, almond, olive oil, safflower, avocado, or any other base of cold-pressed oils. The art and science of aromatherapy involves selecting the proper oils and mixing them in appropriate amounts to obtain the desired effects. We recommend that readers consult with and obtain all preparations made with essential oils from professionals who are experienced in aromatherapy (see Appendix).

USE AND ABUSE OF THE WORD "NATURAL"

Cosmetics and household products containing small amounts of pure, natural ingredients can now be obtained from many sources. However, many manufacturers and producers of foods and cosmetics misuse the word "natural." Some do this innocently or out of ignorance; but others, who are unscrupulous, have jumped on the natural products bandwagon, so to speak, to enrich themselves at the public's expense. As a result, consumers are becoming disenchanted with so-called "natural products," because they have been misled.

There is a tremendous difference between a pure, natural product and a product that has only some natural ingredients. If only a small fraction of a product's ingredients come from natural sources, it is not really "natural." To determine what products are natural, read the ingredients list: if the first and second ingredients listed are derived from a pure, natural source, the product is truly pure and natural. However, if the natural ingredients appear third or fourth in the list, the word "natural" has been misused.

Nearly all perfumes and cosmetics manufactured today are synthetic. Synthetic products tend to irritate the nervous system by upsetting its delicate balance. Many of the major manufacturers of lipsticks use artificial colorings that have been banned as ingredients in foods because of their toxicity. Although they might contain a few natural ingredients, the main ingredients in most fragrances are synthetic. Because natural essences are absent in their formulas, these products do not carry any vital life force; and, without the life force from natural essences, perfumes and cosmetics have no revitalizing effects.

By and large, the cosmetic industry spends more time and money on packaging and promotion than on the value and quality of a product's ingredients. We, as consumers, must learn how to select products that are truly natural and reject those which are not. If we do not create a demand for pure, natural products, the sources of lifelong health and beauty will continue to elude us.[3]

Endnotes

1. For specific suggestions on diet and nutrition see Chapter 4.

2. Low levels of poisoning can result from extremely high doses (10 to 20 milligrams) of essential oils. The following are some potentially dangerous oils, in descending order of toxicity: wintergreen, sage, anise seed, thyme, lemon, fennel, clove, cinnamon, camphor, and cedarwood.

3. Sources for obtaining cosmetics and household products which are pure, natural, and scientifically tested are listed in the Appendix.

3 CLEANSING: PHYSICAL AND MENTAL HYGIENE

Physical Cleansing

THE MOST IMPORTANT of all life's accomplishments is to establish one's own being as a temple of God. All teachers and masters of life tell us that the body is a temple that houses the spirit or soul. Whenever we visit a church, synagogue, sacred shrine, or temple, we find clean, beautiful environments created by those who worship there. In the same way, we should venerate and care for the body by attending to its health, cleanliness, form and shape, and aesthetic beauty.

Up until recently, the average human life span was relatively short. In part, this was because urban populations grew so rapidly that health conditions deteriorated. As it became more difficult to find adequate systems to dispose of waste materials and to control daily hygiene, one result was periodic epidemics of the plague, cholera, and typhus.

Modern western civilization has done much to improve health conditions by creating a vastly more hygienic environment. But even though the average human life span continues to increase as a result of new disease-controlling agents, the unforeseen side effects of these agents present new dangers.

The majority of people have not understood that our

consumption of impurities is a primary cause of disease today. We have forgotten that internal hygiene is as important as creating hygienic conditions outside of the body. Modern society has focused so much on external hygiene that we have not developed habits conducive to maintaining a hygienic environment within the body.

Beauty and good health can only be maintained if the assimilating and eliminating processes in the body are in balance. If we want to slow down the aging process and expand our life span, we must use systematic and scientific methods. This means regulating our breathing and eating patterns, engaging in daily exercises, regularly visiting doctors who specialize in nutrition and natural cleansing techniques, and adopting a regular practice of self-motivating and positive thinking patterns.

To understand the body's eliminating processes, we must recognize that the body has basic needs in food and oxygen, which produce chemical energy. The food we eat is composed of three basic elements: protein, which contains amino acids; fats, which contain the fatty acids; and carbohydrates. (Physical nourishment is discussed in Chapter 4.) These elements are taken in and expelled by the body in a continuous cycle.

This cycle involves a beautiful interplay of relationships through which all beings in the mineral, plant, and animal kingdoms depend upon one another for existence. Because we are made of the same substances as our planet, we need all parts of the planet to exist. For example, minerals, which are an earth element, are essential to the proper functioning of the human body. However, our cells cannot manufacture minerals for themselves, but must absorb them through the foods we eat. This is why salt from the sea is so important in our diet, as are other minerals such as zinc, calcium, and phosphorus, to name only a few. Because minerals come from the earth, they keep us grounded and provide the balancing link between ourselves and the mineral kingdom.

Just as we need to achieve a balanced state between ourselves and the external world, it is the function of the body's assimilation and eliminating systems to maintain a proper balance of the basic ingredients in the body. For example, the human body contains about one quart of oxygen in the blood. The heart pumps blood through the body, and the blood carries oxygen in and carbon dioxide out of every blood cell. It is the lungs, however, that continuously remove carbon dioxide and other impurities from the body. If waste materials are not exhaled properly, they build up in the body, disturbing the body's natural chemistry. This is why proper breathing practices are extremely important. In one year an average adult takes in about four to five tons of oxygen, but only about one thousand pounds are utilized. Diaphragmatic breathing assures that all the wastes are disposed of through exhalation. It is not only what we breathe that is important, but how we breathe.

In ancient literature and scriptures the vital life force and breath were inextricably linked. The human being was seen as the cosmos in microcosm: the body was viewed as "gravity," or "earth," made up of earth substances, and the spirit was seen as "ether," or "heaven," made up of vaporous substances. For this reason, it was said, we leave the body on earth when we die.

BOWEL MANAGEMENT AND COLON CLEANSING

The bowels and colon are the largest cleansing organs in the body's lower region. Partially digested food material is treated in the stomach, liver, pancreas, and kidneys, then passes through the small intestine, and finally enters the large intestine or the colon. *Chyme*, a mixture of water, intestinal secretions, undigested, and indigestible substances, is gradually turned into faecal matter in the colon. This is the last lap of the digestive tract.

An unbalanced diet causes the bowels and colon to work sluggishly. Waste material is not properly expelled and toxins back up into the blood stream. Other excretory organs, like the skin, kidneys, liver, and lungs, are also affected by an unbalanced diet and can become polluted, overworked, and eventually defective. Constipation is one example of this process.

Constipation is often caused by the imperfection and/or an imbalance in the foods we eat. Modern food processing is largely to blame for our dietary deficiencies. For example, in earlier times, when wheat was harvested and milled, the entire kernel was used. In processing wheat today the outer layers, which are rich in vitamins, minerals, and protein, are removed and then fed to animals. The inner part of the wheat is chemically processed and bleached, producing what we call white flour. Part of the processing is to add chemicals and additives to compensate for the natural minerals and nutrients lost in removing the outer layers of bran. Ironically, this adding of synthetic materials is called enrichment. Most bakeries today sell only breads made with refined white flour. These bakery goods are aesthetically pleasing; yet, if we add water to bleached and refined white flour, the result is glue. (In earlier times wallpaper was hung with this glue formula, and in some historic homes such wallpaper still hangs.) Imagine how quantities of white bread, pastry, and donuts consumed over a period of years will act in our intestines!

The western world is dominated by the "instant food habit," and the result is that thousands of people suffer from chronic bowel problems. Proper nutrition includes whole, unprocessed foods, foods that provide an alkaline and acid balance and without chemicals, additives, and preservatives. Only such "pure" foods can be thoroughly assimilated and eliminated by the body.

A diet of unbalanced and impure foods contaminates the bowels, and congested bowels can pollute the entire body. The first symptom of bowels that are not cleansing properly is gray-colored skin. Acne and other skin irritations and diseases are also generally related to the improper functioning of the bowels. The skin is an organ that eliminates but does not assimilate moisture. We know that dry, wrinkled skin needs moisture, but moisturizing the skin will only affect its outer layers. To rejuvenate skin cells, an adequately balanced diet of fresh, whole foods and regular bowel cleansing must be part of our daily routine.

Other symptoms related to congested bowels include the following: stretch marks, cellulite, liver spots, dry, brittle bones, spine deformations, arthritis, rheumatism, cholesterol build-up, and hardening of the arteries, which limits the blood supply to the brain and slows down cellular reproduction.

KIDNEYS, LIVER, AND BLOOD CLEANSING

The kidneys remove waste products from the body by producing urine. They also regulate the amount of water, acid, and salts in the body, eliminate drugs and toxins, and produce some hormones for the regulation of the circulatory system. The kidneys can be called the body's all-purpose filters or purifiers.

The liver plays an important role in maintaining the body's nutrient balance. Almost all nutrients from the digestive tract pass through the liver to be processed on the way to the bloodstream. The liver not only filters the blood, removing wastes and toxins, it also balances the flow of sugar and nutrients to the body. The latter is such an important function that Dr. Rudolph Ballentine, author of *Diet and Nutrition,* calls the liver "the strategic link between nutrition and the mind." The liver, says Dr. Ballentine, "contributes greatly to one's ability to maintain a sense of equanimity, calm, and peace of mind."[1] Some of the more serious liver dysfunctions include jaundice, cirrhosis, anemia, and hepatitis; but daily stresses can also affect the liver. Overeating, worry, and rumination can strain the liver and cause the activity of the digestive system to slow down or become imbalanced.

The bloodstream carries oxygen, hormones, glucose, and other essential substances to every cell in the human body and removes carbon dioxide and other waste products to be discarded through the kidneys and lungs. The circulatory system is the body's main transport highway, and it carries both pure and impure substances to all of the cleansing and nourishing organs. It is closely connected with the sympathetic nervous system, which regulates the rate at which blood flows through the body. As nerve impulses cause the arteries to expand, blood flow increases in the body, and as the arteries contract, blood flow decreases. By constantly reacting to these nerve impulses, the blood is sent wherever it is needed in the body. For example, when we exercise, blood flow to the limbs increases, and when we eat, blood is sent to the stomach and other digestive organs.

High blood pressure, or hypertension, coronary heart artery spasm and arterial sclerosis, and hardening of the arteries are only a few of the aging diseases that can result when the circulatory system becomes polluted or stressed. Researchers have found that improper diet, lack of exercise, worry, and negative thinking all contribute to these disorders. The science of healthy living involves correcting these types of imbalances before irreversible damage occurs.

Cleansing techniques should be gentle so that the body's own natural cleansing systems are enhanced and not strained. As we all know, it is easier to clean house daily rather than once a year, in the spring. Just so, it is far better to establish and maintain a routine of daily cleansing in the body than occasionally to attempt major overhauls. We recommend that three basic cleansing principles be followed: 1) proper diet, 2) adequate physical exercise, and 3) regulation of the breathing patterns. These are all natural processes in the functioning of a healthy body.

A proper diet not only nourishes but also cleanses the body by regulating the digestive and excretory processes. Everything we eat is either: 1) broken down as energy by the body's complex biochemical system, 2) retained in the body as cellular toxins, or 3) expelled as waste material. Therefore, everything we put into the body should be pure and nutritious to obtain the maximum amount of energy from food without overworking the digestive and eliminating systems. There are certain foods such as wheat, dairy, and sweets which, if taken too frequently or in large amounts over a period of time, tend to produce an overabundance of mucous in the nose, sinuses, and the digestive tract. Although mucus is essential, too much mucous creates what we might call intestinal sludge, which slows down the digestive process. Sluggish digestion can cause intestinal gas in the short term together with long-term symptoms such as skin irritations and discolorations, offensive body odors, and chronic constipation.

In addition to eating nutritious food, we should also eat at regular intervals each day. In this way the body becomes accustomed to digesting food at certain times and sets up its own regular patterns of elimination.

If we experiment by taking in fewer calories, we notice that the body's cleansing mechanisms continue to function. The result of a reduction in food intake, or a fast, is that the toxins and waste residues that build up in tissues and in the blood stream are drained out of the body. After fasting we feel lighter physically and more alert mentally. However, using frequent or lengthy fasts as a cleansing technique is not recommended. For most people, an occasional day or two of simply eating less, abstaining from rich, sweet, or heavy foods, or drinking fresh fruit and vegetable juices can cleanse the digestive system. The best fast for the body is from dinner in the evening until breakfast (break-fast) the next morning. This twelve to fourteen hour fast is a perfect opportunity for the body to cleanse itself every day.

Physical exercise and movement are also essential to maintaining regular cleansing. Exercise increases the blood flow and the movement of fluids throughout the body so that wastes, which might otherwise be deposited between cells or in tissues, are loosened up and can be carried out of the body. The stretching exercises described in Chapter 5 are particularly helpful for loosening muscles. Jogging and aerobic exercise are important for stimulating and cleansing the cardiovascular and nervous systems and maintaining muscular tone. Another benefit known to all who exercise regularly is that the mind tends to feel refreshed, "cleaner," less clogged with negativity, and more flexible and creative.

Breathing supports all of the body's metabolic processes and rids the body of carbon dioxide. The breath is one of the most important cleansing tools, because it affects all of the body's organs and tissues. Specific breathing techniques that cleanse and nourish the body in a continuously rejuvenating cycle are described later in this chapter. Laboratory studies show that unless the lower lobes of the lungs are adequately used in breathing the lungs cannot efficiently ventilate the body.

SINUS CLEANSING

The sinuses are air spaces in the bones bordering the nasal cavity. They are lined with mucous membranes, which help to condition the air entering through the nostrils. These membranes help moderate the temperature and humidity of inhaled air and trap some of the incoming dust and bacteria. When the digestive and excretory systems are not throwing off waste products efficiently, the body eliminates some of these residues in nasal mucus. At these times the quality of the mucus changes from normal to too thick or too liquid, depending upon the type of waste material being sloughed off. If the mucous discharge continues, irritation and inflammation of the sinuses can result. Inside the nose there are three scroll-like structures on each side called turbinates. When dry, crusted mucus collects in these fold areas, the passageways to the sinuses become blocked and sinus irritations begin. However, sinus problems can be significantly reduced with the daily practice of an exercise we call the *nasal wash*. Warm, lightly salted water is prepared in a specially designed nasal pot, or neti pot.[2] From the spout of the nasal pot the salt water solution is poured into one nostril and flows out the other. The nasal wash dissolves and washes away excess mucus and allows the sinuses to drain properly. This practice has the same natural effect as washing the sinuses with salty tears. The nasal wash should be practiced in the morning after bathing activities. Many who regularly use this simple cleansing technique find that their colds and sinusitis occur less frequently or are entirely eliminated after only a few months.

BREATH CLEANSING
EXERCISES

If we observe a newborn infant, who has not yet developed poor breathing habits, we will notice breathing patterns different from our own: the breathing is deep and the stomach moves up and down. These are the signs of *diaphragmatic breathing,* the natural and healthy breathing pattern which we, as adults, have forgotten. Like all other muscles, the diaphragm can assume either a contracted or a relaxed position. As it contracts it moves downward, allowing the lungs to fill with air, and as it relaxes it expands and pushes against the lungs, forcing them to exhale.

Breath is the key to life. Since ancient times, the breath has been associated with vitality and health. Breath is also the bridge between the mind and body. When the breath is calm the mind is calm and vice-versa. However, the minute our

FIGURE 3.1:

Diaphragmatic breathing

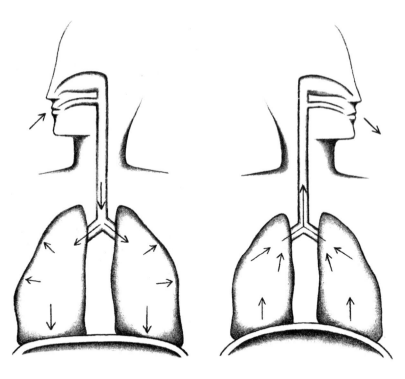

breathing is interrupted there is also a break, change, or disturbance in our thoughts. A steady, calm mind that is well directed and focused is accompanied by a calm, smooth breath pattern. The breath, then, is the mind's natural tranquilizer.

The life force, prana, or chi, is the vital energy contained not only in the food we eat but also in the air we breathe. Therefore, breathing is not a function just to take in oxygen and eliminate CO_2 but it is a source of vital energy and nourishment as well. Understanding the relationship between the mind and the breath is a complex science. In the ancient tradition of yoga the great teachers, or yogis, trained themselves to become masters in the science of breath. Today, the science of breath is practiced in yoga as well as in other great traditions such as Buddhism, Sophism, mystical Christianity, mystical Judaism, and Taoism. It is also used extensively in the martial arts of Karate, T'ai Chi, Kung Fu and Akido. Participants in modern sports rely on breath control for maximum performance, although they may not be aware of their breath. Because our mental and physical bodies are meant to work in synergistic harmony, it is essential that we, too, study the science of breath.

If we were to do a survey of breathing patterns among adult men and women, we would discover that the majority of people breathe shallowly, using only the upper part of their lungs most of the time. The Architect who designed the human body designed it perfectly and gave us upper and lower lungs for balanced, complete breathing. However, with the stresses and pressures of modern living we have developed many unhealthy habits, among them the unconscious habit of upper chest breathing. This form of breathing is characterized by short, shallow breaths, panting, jerks in the breath, and pauses between breaths. When we breathe in this way we are using mostly the middle and upper parts of the lungs. Neglecting the lower lungs eventually causes them to become "lazy"; and the effects of "lazy breathing" are especially evident whenever we are under stress. Our breaths are particularly shallow, rapid, and irregular when we are hurried, angry, nervous, or upset in any way. At the same time we feel that we "can't think straight." This is because chest breathing is not an energy-efficient method of mixing air and blood in the lungs, requiring many short breaths so that the blood becomes oxygenated. The heart, then, must work harder. As the breath pattern speeds up and becomes irregular, the brain receives nervous signals from the lungs and chest that elicits a flight or fight reflex. This arousal releases adrenalin and prepares the mind and body for physical survival. Establishing a constant reflex pattern leads to excessive anxiety and emotional stress. Hence we cannot focus our thoughts, take in information appropriately, or respond in a calm and collected manner. The internal organs may cease to work appropriately, resulting in diseases of hypertension, coronary artery disease, stomach ulcers, colitis, and numerous other ailments. These are truly psychosomatic diseases brought on by stress. Yet stress is caused by chronic erratic breathing; thereby stress begets stress.

Despite claims to the contrary in the literature on stress management, stress cannot be managed without managing the breath. Changing our breathing habits is like changing any other habit. We create obstacles to improvement by not committing ourselves to change and by failing to believe in the importance of proper breathing. Healthy breathing techniques have been taught according to scientifically proven methods to thousands of persons at the Himalayan International Institute, a research and educational center in Honesdale, Pennsylvania. (Institute researchers, headed by Dr. Rudolph Ballentine and Dr. John Clarke, have developed a computerized instrument that measures the relationship of particular breathing patterns to various physical disorders.)

The following practices, which are being taught widely at such holistic health clinics and research centers, will help us regulate and balance the breath and, thereby, cleanse and nourish the entire body. The techniques outlined here should be practiced consciously and daily at regular times. This practice routine should be maintained throughout our lives in order to regain our naturally good breathing habits and then to ensure the continuous revitalization of our physical and mental bodies.

Diaphragmatic breathing

Of all the breathing exercises described in this chapter, diaphragmatic breathing is the most important. We recommend the following simple techniques for establishing diaphragmatic breathing.

Lie on your back on a blanket, mat, or rug with one hand resting on your chest and the other on the lower edge of the rib cage where the abdomen begins. As you inhale, feel the lower edge of the rib cage expand and the abdomen rise; as you exhale, feel this area contract. There should be little, if any, movement in the chest. Inhalation and exhalation should be regular, smooth, and even in length. Do this practice for fifteen minutes in the morning before getting out of bed and again before falling asleep. It will help you begin the day with a relaxed attitude and calm you in preparation for sleep.

To learn diaphragmatic breathing, place a large book on the abdomen. On inhalation the book rises and on exhalation the book falls. Gradually try to incorporate this method of breathing into your daily life so that it becomes natural and is done without thinking.

Two-to-one

A breath exer...
effect is called t...
increases the acti...
— the body's relax...
speed up digestion,...
body. This exercise i...
or in times of stress to...

First, establish smooth...
make your exhalations tw...
may begin by mentally cou...
and "one-two" as you slowly...
to three minutes.

Complete Breath Exercise

To feel more energetic without cre... stress in the body
or mind, we recommend the comple... breath exercise. This
exercise stimulates the sympathetic nervous system, which
prepares the body for action by increasing the heart rate and
moving the blood away from the digestive and excretory
organs to the muscles and limbs. The complete breath exercise
can remove fatigue almost instantaneously and leave you
feeling physically energetic as well as mentally fresh and well
balanced.

Establish diaphragmatic breathing; inhale slowly and
deeply, filling first the lower rib cage, then the chest area, and
finally, the clavicle area. Exhale completely, emptying the
clavicle area, then the chest, and finally, the lower rib cage.
Do this exercise for four to five minutes slowly and systematically, without holding your breath or creating any pauses
between inhalation and exhalation.

Alternate Nostril Breathing

If we place one finger directly below the nose, we will notice
that the flow of breath in one nostril or the other is predominant. Every two to three hours this dominance changes so that
the stream of breath seems to alternate continuously between
the left and right nostril. This natural rhythm can be inter-

by colds, sinusitis, pollutants, irregular eating and sleeping schedules, and even by emotional disturbances. Alternate nostril breathing helps to balance the activities of the autonomic nervous system, that is, its sympathetic (active) and parasympathetic (resting) functions. Those who are adept at this exercise may observe that they feel more active and assertive while breathing through the right nostril and quieter and more introspective while breathing through the left nostril. We believe that there may be a correlation between this breath pattern and the activities of the right and left brain, which are being studied extensively today by medical and educational researchers.

To restore balance to the flow of breath in the right and left nostrils, we recommend what is called the alternate nostril breathing exercise. It should be done after several minutes of practicing diaphragmatic breathing.

Sit comfortably with your head, neck, and trunk in a straight line. Using the right hand, close the right nostril with the right thumb and exhale slowly, evenly, and smoothly. Release the right nostril and, with the third and fourth fingers of the right hand, close the left nostril and inhale in the same slow and even manner. There should be no pauses between inhalation and exhalation. You may want to count slowly from one to four with each inhalation and exhalation to ensure that your breath is even in length. Later, as your breath becomes slower and deeper, you can increase the count to six or eight. Repeat inhalation through the right nostril and exhalation through the left nostril two more times.

When you have repeated this round (inhaling right nostril, exhaling left nostril) three times, exhale completely through the right nostril and, still keeping the left nostril closed, inhale through this same nostril. Begin again, this time inhaling through the right nostril and exhaling through the left nostril. Repeat two more times.

At the end of the exercise you will have completed a cycle consisting of: a) exhaling through the right nostril and inhaling through the left nostril three times, and then, b) inhaling through the right nostril and exhaling through the left nostril three times.

As you practice, you may add another complete breathing cycle to the exercise. Additional cycles will give you an even greater sense of clarity and well-being as the sympathetic and parasympathetic systems come into balance for longer periods of time.

All of these breathing exercises should be practiced daily at regular times. Diaphragmatic breathing should be practiced at least twice a day, upon arising and before going to sleep. The alternate nostril exercise is particularly helpful if practiced just before meals. Incorporating it with the diaphragmatic breathing exercise upon arising and before breakfast can give you a fresh, relaxed start to the day. Two-to-one breathing should be done immediately after morning stretching exercises or following any physical activity or mental stress during the day. The complete breath exercise can be practiced any time you feel fatigued; it will give you a natural and long lasting "high" rather than the jitters created by caffeine and other stimulants.[3]

Once we are physically cleansed, we begin to develop the need for psychological cleansing as well. We start to "clean up our lives," as it were, by becoming aware of the "emotional dirt" that has clogged our minds and prevented our personal growth.

Mental Cleansing

HEALTHY PEOPLE ARE EASY TO RECOGNIZE: they stand straight, speak confidently, their eyes sparkle, and they smile readily. They tell us that they generally feel relaxed and undisturbed, that they are growing continuously, that life is exciting to them, and that their relationships are rewarding. Beneath the external glow of good health in such people is a healthy mind filled with positive thoughts and free from such impurities as fear, anger, and disappointment.

Stress, anxiety, and depression are symptoms of a restless, undirected, and polluted mind. Negative thinking affects our physical health so significantly that it is the primary cause of dis-ease for modern society. However, now there are scientific ways to bring the mind into a state of clarity, wellness, and equipoise.

A healthy mind is constantly expanding and growing. The way to rejuvenate our thought patterns is, first, to analyze how our thoughts affect us and, second, to learn how our thoughts can change those effects and make our lives healthier and more satisfying. There is an old Japanese saying that if we are sitting on a mountain, it is difficult to observe the entire mountain. In the same way, it is difficult to observe ourselves. We cannot see why and how we are causing certain events to occur or how these events are affecting us. Our vision of ourselves is limited because we are not in the habit of taking time out daily to discern the process of cause and effect. Before we can know ourselves and improve our health and our daily lives, we must adopt the habit of steady personal observation.

Daily mental observation and balancing cleanses and rejuvenates the mind. It involves examining thoughts, removing self-destructive thoughts from the mind, and welcoming all life's experiences as opportunities for change and growth. In this school of psychology, thoughts are used to teach us how "it is" and how "it can be."

MENTAL REJUVENATION

The greatest obstacle to mental growth is our own inability to understand and accept reality. We know, in theory, that reality or truth can take many forms; it can be interpreted differently at different times and by different people. Nevertheless, often we get caught up in judging these views of reality, believing one valuable and another worthless. A coin has two faces, one different from the other, yet both faces interpret the true value of the coin. Just so in life: masculine is not superior to feminine; yin is not a better element than yang; and an alkaline state is not preferable to an acidic one. The various aspects of reality simply exist — possessing different properties and characteristics, as pairs of opposites designed to balance each other, and engaging in different activities. But these various aspects cannot be subjected to value judgments. To understand the true science of being we must see the whole phenomenon of reality and every activity in its entirety.

Most of us may agree that reality takes many forms but find

it difficult to identify what is "real" in our daily lives. For example, often when we are conversing with another person we do not really hear what he or she is saying. We get hung up on our interpretation of one or two words and miss the other's real message to us. In this way, we miss out on the infinite possibilities for developing rich and meaningful relationships. All our relationships with the external world are interpreted according to how we view our internal world. We perceive and judge the external world in the same manner that we perceive and judge ourselves. Therefore, when we get upset about someone else's imperfections, we are really reacting to our own imperfections.

We can also become bogged down by self-defeating mental conversations with ourselves. These destructive "self-talks" can become so repetitive that there is no way for new thoughts to enter our minds. Everyday we are constantly barraged with information — messages, suggestions, and cues — about ourselves and others. We can choose to take them all in and be influenced and even confused by them, or we can choose to observe them without becoming disturbed, realizing that there are many interpretations of the truth. On the level of material objects, one person sees a modern painting as a great work of art while another person sees it as a monstrosity. We can argue endlessly about such differing opinions or accept them as equally viable notions of the truth. If someone tells us we are stupid but we feel confident of our intellectual capabilities, that statement will not matter. But if we have doubts and insecurities about our intelligence, the other's statement will disturb and even hurt us. On the self-talk level, we notice that when we are depressed or suffering from some mental or physical pain, we see the world differently. We interpret everything at such times through the eyes of pain. Because of our perceptions at that moment, we might not see the Mona Lisa smiling at us, but crying with us.

Depression is the experience of de-pressing the mind's natural positive state. A de-pressed mind is weighed down by anxieties, insecurities, and negative thoughts. There can be no progress or growth if it is held down by the pressures it perceives. A mind contracted by de-pression cannot be relieved of pressure until it learns how to relax, expand, and open itself to new thoughts. Just as the body becomes constipated by feeding it unbalanced and impure food, we can create mental constipation by feeding unbalanced and impure thoughts to the mind and leaving them there to stagnate and putrify. A well-balanced mind can direct its energy away from self-destructive thoughts to positive mental activities. Every day such a mind gives birth to new, healthier, and more expansive goals and affirmations. It becomes more skilled at discriminating which thoughts and activities are wholesome and will promote health and which thoughts and activites are crippling and will create dis-ease. A daily program of mental cleansing is the key to maintaining mental growth and rejuvenation. Mental cleansing is a five-step process which, if used regularly, allows us to direct the law of cause and effect and therefore transform our lives.

RELAXATION   Relaxation is the antidote to stress. Modern researchers have found that many stress-related diseases, such as hypertension, migraine headaches, and digestive disorders, are greatly alleviated or even eliminated when we learn to relax. Based upon numerous recent studies on the causes and effects of chronic tension, nearly all stress-management books, tapes, and programs today begin with a basic relaxation exercise. The state of relaxation is not only physically beneficial, it is also an invaluable preparation for the mental cleansing exercises outlined in this chapter.

Relaxation exercise

The simple yet highly effective relaxation exercise described here can be practiced at any time either by itself or just before any of the mental cleansing techniques. This procedure should be followed to relax, refresh, and revitalize the body and mind.

Lie on your back on a firm yet comfortable surface such as a rug or mat. Spread the legs six to eight inches apart, and rest the arms a few inches from the body with palms upward. Close the eyes and establish diaphragmatic breathing (as described earlier in this chapter). Focusing on a smooth, even breathing pattern, relax systematically from head to toe. Begin at the forehead and relax the eyebrows, eyes, nose, cheeks, and mouth. You may tell yourself mentally to relax each part of the body as you move toward the toes. After relaxing the head and face, move to the neck, shoulders, upper and lower arms, wrists, hands, fingers, and fingertips. Relax back up the arms to the shoulders and then move on to the chest and stomach, all the way down to the toes. Repeat these steps moving upwards from the toes to the forehead. The more this exercise is practiced, the deeper the level of relaxation and the more quickly you will be able to reach the relaxed state. This exercise is not intended to induce sleep but to help relieve mental and physical stress.

Relaxation/tension exercise

Another technique that calms the body and also tones the muscles and autonomic nervous system is the relaxation/tension exercise. Again, lying on the back with legs comfortably apart and arms at the sides with palms up, bring your attention to the right leg. Consciously tense the toes and point them away from the body without tensing any other part of the leg. Gradually tense the entire leg, beginning with the foot and moving upward to the ankle, calf, knee, and thigh. Breathe diaphragmatically and try to avoid tension in any other part of the body. If you feel any muscles shaking, reduce the tension slightly. Hold the tension briefly and then relax slowly from the toes, following the same order in which you created the tension. Next, tense and relax the left leg in the same systematic order. Repeat the exercise a second time with each leg. Finally, do the exercise with both legs simultaneously. When you are finished, relax completely, breathing in and out several times.

The exercise now focuses on tensing and relaxing the right side of the body. Tense the right leg and right arm simultaneously. The arm should be tensed systematically, beginning with outstretched fingers and moving upwards to the wrist, forearm, elbow, and upper arm. Hold the tension on the right side only and then release the tension in the right arm and leg slowly and systematically. Proceed to the left side of the body, using the same technique. Repeat the exercise on each side and relax completely.

Now, slowly tense, hold, and relax the right arm. Do the same exercise with the left arm. Repeat the exercise with each arm, right and then left. Do the tension/relaxation exercise with both arms simultaneously. Tense both arms again and relax completely.

The last step of this exercise is to tense all the limbs simultaneously. First create tension, then hold the tension and finally relax. Remain in the relaxed position for several minutes, focusing your mind on smooth, even, diaphragmatic breathing. You should feel refreshed and invigorated after this exercise.

GROUNDING   The state of being "grounded" has many different names. It has been called centering, the state of contemplation, the state of meditation, the state of prayer, and the state of peace or at-one-ness. It is that state of being in which we are the most relaxed and the most creative.

Before we can describe the grounding exercises, we must explain how and why they are effective. The mind and the nervous system are the body's receivers of information. We know that the mind records and stores all of a person's thoughts and experiences. We also know that the body's nervous system receives messages, impulses, or vibrations and carries them through the spinal cord to the brain. The autonomic nervous system is that part of the body's structure of nerves which generally is not under our voluntary control. It is divided into two parts: the sympathetic and the parasympathetic systems. The sympathetic nerves stimulate the body's involuntary "action" muscles; for example, to increase heart and lung activity, constrict blood vessels in the skin, and coordinate the bladder and rectal muscles. The parasympathetic nerves control the opposite involuntary muscle activities to lower the heart rate, slow down breathing, relax sphincter muscles, and so on. The sympathetic system speeds up the activities of the involuntary muscles (a yang effect), while the parasympathetic system relaxes those activities (a yin effect).

Each of the systems must act at exactly the appropriate moment. If balance between the two systems is not maintained, one or the other will be overworked or "stressed." Sooner or later, this imbalance will lead to dis-ease in the digestive, circulatory, or respiratory systems.

The nervous system and the mind are like electronic receivers, picking up hundreds of thousands of impulses or vibrations every few minutes. As with any other electronic instrument, the mind must be properly grounded. If a radio, stereo, or television set is not grounded, there will be static or interference with the sound or image. The vibrations will be transmitted to the speaker or the screen in a scattered, unrecognizable way, and the listener will miss the message altogether. Similarly, unless the mind is grounded, the vibrations it receives and the messages, cues, and data it absorbs will also be distorted. This can be illustrated by the following graph. At the top of the graph (10) is the pattern of vibrations as they are received by the mind when it is in a disturbed, agitated, or ungrounded state. The further we go toward the bottom of the graph, the grounded state, the more settled and undisturbed the vibrations, until at 1, the grounded level, the message is singular and clear.

It is essential, then, that the mind be able to coordinate and balance these vibrations so that reception is clear, sharp, and fine-tuned. Actually, "getting high" is coming down to the grounded state where we are relaxed and receptive enough to hear the real message, or the truth.

Grounding exercise

Grounding is the first exercise in mental cleansing and it should be practiced once in the morning, once in the evening, and throughout the day before embarking on any important activity. As we discussed earlier in this chapter, the breath is the body's natural tranquilizer. The mind and breath act in parallel, so when the breath is calm, the mind will also be calm.

To begin the grounding exercise, sit in a comfortable position in a quiet space free from activities which will distract

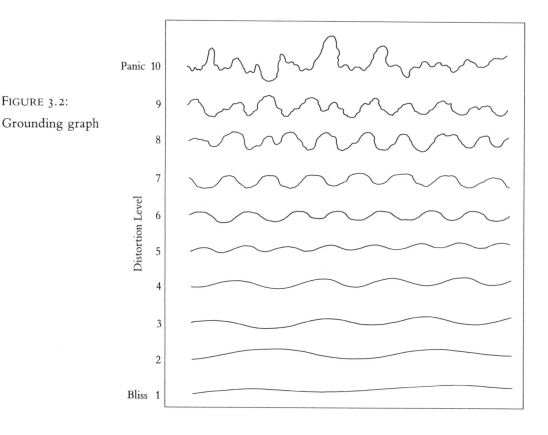

FIGURE 3.2:

Grounding graph

you. Relax your entire body and breathe quietly and diaphragmatically without any pauses or jerks between breaths.

Next, let your eyelids close and concentrate on focusing the breath and mind together. To do this, think of one thought as you slowly inhale and one thought as you exhale. You may choose the words "peace and harmony," "love and ease," or any combination of words or sounds that makes you feel calm and serene. In this relaxed state, you are a witness or spectator. All the mind's videotapes, as it were, of thoughts, activities, and experiences will be replayed before you. The more relaxed and grounded you are, the clearer and more in-focus the pictures on the screen of the mind.

Practicing consciously and calmly for even five minutes will ground us; practicing for ten minutes will ground us deeper; and the longer and more frequently we practice, the more grounded we become. If we practiced all the time, we could be grounded all the time! However, because changing our habits is a gradual process, we need to practice grounding daily, on a regular basis. We recommend this exercise be done at least twice a day — once in the morning upon arising and after bathing but before breakfast, and once in the evening before bed. It is also helpful to do a short grounding practice at mid-day or before any major change in routine and particularly before any stressful activity. Grounding will help us prepare for an upcoming event so that we participate with complete attention, perform well, and take in and respond to information appropriately.

One of the major benefits of grounding is that it allows us to review our past activities and experiences and lets us learn how to create new, healthier, and more rewarding ones. For example, let us say that we had an appointment to meet someone. We planned and prepared for the appointment, but the other person failed to show up. We had made a mental "appointment" and, therefore, became "dis-appointed," and perhaps even angry, when our expectations were not fulfilled. The grounding exercise can be used to eliminate a negative reaction to such an occurrence. By replaying the mental tape of that experience, we can analyze how we caused our own "disappointment" and other counterproductive feelings. Perhaps we heard only certain words of the other person's message, signaling to us that a meeting definitely was going to occur when, in fact, the other intended a chance get-together.

Through grounding, we can also replay the event to teach us how to act differently next time; in other words, how to cause different effects. This is the essence of mental growth and rejuvenation. Using our missed appointment example, during the grounding exercise we might realize that the other person may not have intentionally missed the appointment. It is possible that he or she was detained or forgot the appointment. Since this also has happened to us, it is understandable. A mix-up simply occurred. There is nothing disturbing about it, it is what happened, it is reality. Now that we have chosen a positive emotional response, we are free to explore all the alternatives for future action.

Modern society has programmed itself to escape from and suppress pain. If we have a headache, we take aspirin; if we have a stomachache, we take antacids. Pain is the effect of some imbalance, and by covering up the pain we avoid looking within ourselves to discover the cause of the pain. Unless we confront the cause of pain and dis-ease, the learning or growing process is incomplete. Pain exists only as a signal telling us that we are doing something incorrectly. To ignore or suppress these signals is to miss life's most valuable lesson: the discovery of reality, or truth, which is shown to us through the law of cause and effect. This is the domain of self-discovery where real learning begins.

In a similar view, "wrong" only exists to be made "right." Many of us are preoccupied with what is right and wrong. We fail to understand that wrong is as important as right because, without wrong, there can be no right! What we think of as wrong is actually the seed that grows into the right way of acting and being. When we realize this, the process of forgiving or letting go becomes easy. We can free ourselves from blaming and be grateful for the lesson learned from our wrong actions or attitudes. Just as we can see the cup half-empty or half-full, we can see wrong not as punishment but as a lesson for growth.

By practicing grounding exercises, the possibilities for personal expansion are infinite. There is no area of life, no activity, no relationship, and no thought that cannot be transformed, rejuvenated, and made more healthy and purposeful with regular practice of the grounding exercise.

CHRONOLOGICAL MENTAL INVENTORY

In the beginning of any new practice in life we should assess where we are. In the first stages of mental cleansing, we recommend making an inventory of past and present mental activities. In this way we can step back or away from "the mountain" in the Japanese saying alluded to earlier, and take stock of our attitudes, our likes and dislikes, and our lives in general. On a sheet of paper make two columns. In the left hand column list everything you don't like about your life: places and people; things about your friends, associates and yourself; as well as responsibilities and the activities in which you participate. In the right hand column list everything you like about your life and all of your desires, goals, and dreams.

Write as much as you can and do not withhold or deny yourself anything in formulating the inventory. You may continue to add to the list over several weeks to finish the inventory.

When completed, the inventory provides insight into our own past, present, and future as they appear to us. By objectively studying the inventory, we will soon realize a most interesting phenomenon: All of our personal strengths show up on the inventory as what we like about ourselves and others, while all of our fears, insecurities, and weaknesses, which we deny, show up as aspects of ourselves and others that we dislike. By analyzing our recorded likes and dislikes listed on the inventory, we can face our strengths and weaknesses realistically. If we do not like a particular activity or person, it is because our own insecurities are mirrored by that mental image and we react with distaste to what we see. If we are not satisfied with events as they occur and recur in our lives, it is because we are reacting improperly to them. Mahatma Gandhi once said: "All the devils exist in our own hearts. That's where all battles have to be fought." Everything we see in the external world is a reflection or projection of our internal state of being. We need to reprogram our responses, but first we need a thorough mental inventory to show us who and where we are.

MENTAL GOAL SETTING   One of our greatest gifts is the ability to change. If, after analyzing our past and present lives, we see things that we don't like, we can develop a strategy for change. On the other hand, if we see that our strengths can and should be expanded, we can add them as well to our strategy for personal growth. The process of developing strategies for growth is based upon goal setting.

One's personal life and the life of a corporation are remarkably similar. Life is a business, and it is called the business of being here. All successful corporations achieve their goals through a process called strategic planning. Strategic planning is a commitment to activity. The first step is to analyze where we are and how we got there. In business, for example, we might ask, "What caused this particular company to go into the red?" Next we would ask, "What needs to be changed to put the company in the black, and how long will this take?" As the company grows and expands, its objectives will change. In the same way, our personal goals will change over time, and this is why people, like businesses, need to constantly review and update their goals based upon what they have learned.

From the mental inventory discussed in the previous section, we can choose specific goals that we want to accomplish, which will relieve stress and help us become healthier and enjoy life more. However, instead of setting goals that will teach us more about reality and truth, most of us choose ways to escape from reality. To relieve stress and dis-ease we must identify what causes them; and we can only do this through inner activity, that is, through the process of self-conversation and self-confrontation. External activities only lead us away from inner truth. For example, for someone who is under stress, playing tennis is physically beneficial, relaxing, and even meditative, some say. It is helpful insofar as it momentarily takes us away from our present thought patterns; but playing tennis does not reveal to us the cause of our stress. The game of tennis tells us nothing more than we already know about the game of life: we enjoy it when we win but not when we lose. However, if after playing tennis we analyze why we behaved as we did on the court, we can learn something about ourselves. For example, our forehand and backhand strokes may tell us something about our right and left brain thinking processes. It is important after any outward activity, whether at the office or at home, to do some inner analysis. This is the only way to learn what caused certain events and how to effect different or better results.

All of our goal setting and strategic planning should be based upon our inner search for self-knowledge, for knowing the self leads to self-rejuvenation. Our list of goals should be reviewed frequently. It is important to separate goals that are short term from those which are long term. Some goals may be accomplished in one week or one month, while others may take a year or even an entire lifetime. If our vision is too narrow and too many of our goals are short term, the pressure to achieve them will build and only produce greed, more stress, and ultimate failure. We are unable to resolve our problems, whether individually or societally, because we are accustomed to instant solutions: instant food, instant success, instant enlightenment. In our daily diets, instant coffee is no longer real coffee because of its chemical additives; instant

FIGURE 3.3:   Sample mental inventory list

Things I don't like		Things I want to accomplish
Being overweight	1	Get into shape
Renting an apartment	5	Buy a house
Taking the bus	2	Buy a car
People who steal	5	Financial Security
My job		Family / wife, marriage
Judging Others		Travel / world
Being in debt	11	Pay off loans
Fear		College, higher education
Stress	15	Open a Café
Bills		
Jealous people		
Smoking		

breakfast is not solid food but a liquid filled with synthetic additives; and instant banana shakes are not even made with real bananas!

True success can only be achieved with patience, long-term goals, and scientifically researched, directed, and guided activities. Therefore, after identifying our goals, we can think realistically and logically about which ones can be reached this year. Circle them and mark them as number one goals. Next, find goals that can be accomplished in two years. Circle them and mark them as number two goals. By following the same order for goals to be reached in three, four, five years, and so on, we can plan our entire lives.

Once our desires have been identified and categorized into long- and short-term goals, we should find and surround ourselves with people who have achieved the same goals. These people are known as mentors, teachers, or even masters. A mentor is one who practices what he or she teaches and who can help us design strategies for attaining our goals. Mentors, or teachers, are essential if life is to be lived properly. Just as all teachers encourage their students to practice, so, too, the exercises of grounding, taking inventory, and setting goals must be practiced daily if we are to change and grow.

DAILY MENTAL INVENTORY

Laziness is the root of all evil. Therefore, we need to develop a daily system with which to confront our laziness directly. Self-motivation can be generated through a scientific and systematic process. However, self-motivation should never be applied with force. It involves thinking in a relaxed and logical manner so that we can analyze ourselves and our path of action and be directed by the true inner guide, the self. By practicing the techniques described in this section daily, self-motivation will become a natural response of the subconscious mind. Personal development will no longer be painful but rather joyful and rewarding. In this section we describe activities that are conducive to maintaining a productive life schedule and their underlying principles. In Chapter 6 we describe how much time should be apportioned to these activities.

To be truly effective in life, we should analyze our activities by 1) conducting a daily mental inventory; and 2) measuring our progress against our stated goals, which can be business or personal goals or contributions to society. If we are not reaching our goals, or not reaching them fast enough, or if the goals are not inherently positive, we punish ourselves subconsciously; and a self-destructive state of mind leads to physical or mental dis-ease. Some of the dis-eases of the mind (often manifested in our attitudes) that block self-motivation include: indifference, indecision, worry, procrastination, complaining, faith without action, lack of discipline. Every time we encounter in ourselves one of these attitudinal dis-eases, we can counteract it with the following thoughts and activities:

- Indifference: This attitude indicates that we cannot discriminate between what should and should not be done. To develop discrimination, we should begin looking for the positive everywhere and in everything.

- Indecision: Without making decisions we will never learn which activities are right or wrong for us. We can only learn what is correct for us by doing, that is, through direct experience.

- Worry: This is an emotion related to fear. Fear and worry are caused by ignorance, or not having the necessary information to be fully prepared. Worry can be eliminated by 1) getting enough information before starting an activity, 2) practicing and perfecting our skills so that we are comfortable performing an activity, and 3) putting faith and confidence in our skills and in the activity once it is begun. When worry extends to circumstances beyond our control it is time to surrender to the higher power. Accept reality as it exists, knowing that you are part of nature and nature can appear cruel at times. Nourish yourself through acceptance instead of torturing yourself.

- Procrastination: This is a by-product of indecision and worry. The solution is to tell ourselves, "Don't start tomorrow, start now." The sooner we start, the sooner we will learn what is right and wrong for us.

- Complaining: This attitude poisons ourselves and others, and complaining repetitively is a mental dis-ease that eventually can cause physical dis-ease. We can stop complaining by analyzing our own weaknesses and beginning to work on ourselves.

- Faith without action: Faith without action is useless. Our faith must be supported with realistic goals and sensible long-term strategies to achieve those goals.

- Lack of discipline: To master our weaknesses we must learn discipline, which means being steady and reliable and holding ourselves accountable for our actions. Without discipline we will remain weak. Therefore, our two choices are the pain of discipline or the pain of regret.

Once we have removed the blocks to self-motivation, the following techniques can be used daily as part of an on-going process of personal growth and evolution:

1. Set goals daily and visualize your goals accomplished in a clear way. Picture the fulfillment of your desires now and feel the joy and restfulness that comes with visualizing your realized goals. Visualize yourself in brilliant health, eating pure foods, and thinking pure thoughts. Practice this daily goal-setting along with the grounding exercise in the morning, when you are relaxed and fresh.

2. Avoid all stressful efforts and impatience in goal setting, strategic planning, and in all thoughts and activities. Remember that the thankful heart is always close to the riches of the universe.

3. Seek out your mentor for advice frequently and use tried and proven techniques to accomplish your goals.

4. Make a mental inventory daily. This will be a short form of the inventory described earlier in this chapter and should be done in the evening to review all of the day's activities. Ask yourself what things you liked and disliked, whether your goals for the day were met, and why or why not.

AFFIRMATION Affirming ourselves and affirming our goals should be done every morning along with the grounding and goal-setting exercises. Whenever we doubt our capabilities, we create an instant block to achieving our goals and we can only hope for success. There is a vast difference between hope and knowledge: one who hopes is still hoping to know; he or she doesn't know yet. One who knows can be confident that all of his or her goals will be reached.

Two techniques will help in self-affirmation: the *eidetic* (seeing) exercise and the *kinesthetic* (feeling) exercise. Practicing affirmations eidetically means that we can actually visualize the image of the affirmation. Practicing kinesthetically means that we can imagine how it would feel to be the person in our affirmation. These techniques are exercises involing no movement. They train our "thought muscles" in somewhat the same way that we have discovered how to train the autonomic nervous system.[4]

FIGURE 3.4:   Thinking affirmation

Using both the eidetic and kinesthetic approaches, calmly and confidently see and feel yourself as you want to be. As examples, you might make any of the following affirmations:

I am patient.
I am calm.
I am capable.
I am intelligent.
I am beautiful.
I am at peace.

The word "no" does not exist in the vocabulary of affirmations. Negative statements like "I will not be impatient," or doubtful statements like "I hope I will be patient," are not affirming. Rather, see and feel yourself acting in a particular way, and know and believe that it will happen that way.

The benefits of affirmation are the same as if we had actually performed an activity successfully or acted the way we desired. This is because when we practice affirmations with imagery and feeling, we produce a mental result that becomes our reality. Thus, we are bound to be successful because we have programmed ourselves for success.

THE LETTING-GO PROCESS This final exercise in the process of mental cleansing should be done in the evening with the grounding and daily inventory exercises. If one of our important goals was not met during the day we might feel disturbed, depressed, disappointed, or angry at ourselves or at people who interfered. How do we relieve this stress? We can suppress it with alcohol or drugs, overeat, or watch television to escape our unpleasant feelings. Or we can quiet ourselves with the grounding exercise, focus our mind on the breath, and play back the day's events as they really happened. In this calm state we can see all sides of the situation and evaluate what really did happen. We will see that we allowed ourselves to become upset because we were attached to our own particular interpretation of the truth. What happened was not our fault or anyone else's. If we blame ourselves and others for unsatisfying effects, we can never learn what really caused the activity to go awry.

The truth is that our expectations or goals, if realistic ones, were not met simply because we did not have enough information. Additional or more accurate information could have prepared us better or protected us from the unfortunate result. Criticizing others or condemning ourselves is useless, so we should let go of our negative thoughts and forgive ourselves and others. Ultimately the real purpose of every activity in life is to help us grow. Each activity is another source for accumulating information so that we can understand reality more clearly and improve our lives.

The mental exercises described in this chapter are designed to cleanse the mind and to keep it in balance. A well-balanced mind learns how to use the past to effect change for the future. One who practices these exercises remains calm or grounded, makes a daily inventory of experiences, sets daily goals and affirms them, and lets go of non-productive or destructive thoughts. These exercises, along with the exercises for physical cleansing, continuously rejuvenate the body and mind.

Endnotes

1. *Diet and Nutrition,* Rudolph Ballentine, Himalayan Publishers, Honesdale, PA, 1982.

2. A source for obtaining the neti pot appears in the Appendix.

3. The time management skills outlined in Chapter 4 will demonstrate how to incorporate these cleansing techniques into a daily routine of vitalizing activities.

4. *Exercise Without Movement,* by Swami Rama, cited in the Suggested Reading List, is a recently published practical guide to physical exercises that control the involuntary nervous system.

4 NOURISHING THE BODY AND MIND

Daily Physical Nutrition

WE ARE ABLE TO PRESERVE YOUTH, health, and beauty when the body's cells are nourished with the life-force — prana or chi — contained in pure foods. Only when properly nourished, can the body's cells repair and reproduce. Aging begins when we do not receive enough of this pure, wholesome nourishment. If we eat impure foods and have imbalanced diets early in life, the aging process will begin prematurely. Therefore, it is essential that we nourish our bodies in a systematic and scientific way.

The philosophical basis for the science of nutrition was laid nearly three thousand years ago in China. As spelled out in the literature of that period, everything in the universe is governed by pairs of opposites. For example, there is no heat without cold, no alkaline without acid, and no lightness without heaviness. Further, all pairs of opposites arise from the fundamental polarity between yin and yang. In this philosophy, yin and yang must be in balance for harmony to exist in the universe and on earth. Therefore, foods with the highest nutritional value are those with a proper balance of yin and yang qualities. Lighter foods, such as fruits and raw vegetables, are examples of yin foods; beef, pork, and other heavy foods have more yang qualities. Generally, foods that have the best balance between yin and yang qualities are whole grains and cooked vegetables. Foods that are extremely yin, such as sugar, or extremely yang, such as red meat, should be eaten in moderation. Other factors, like weather or the seasons, should also be considered in selecting yin and yang foods. Summer, for example, is thought of as a season with yang qualities, and it is better, therefore, to eat more yin foods, such as fruits and light vegetables. In winter, which is considered yin, heavier foods, such as whole grains and cooked vegetables, are recommended.

Viewed from this perspective, nutrition has a deeper meaning. Selecting foods should be more than looking at a chart and counting calories, protein, and vitamin requirements; and preparing foods should not just be a haphazard combination of pre-packaged, instant, or processed ingredients. Instead, nutrition is meant to be a scientific method for maintaining physical and mental harmony and equilibrium.

There is no such thing as one universal diet. Every individual has his or her own dietary needs and rhythms caused by different imbalances or dis-eases that require special attention. In the science of nutrition the law of cause and effect is easy to observe: some people develop food allergies, most people get a high from caffeine or sugar, and anyone can get an upset stomach from eating spoiled or contaminated food. However, most of us have no idea what special nutrients we need because we have never studied our eating habits.

The best way to determine our nutritional needs is to keep a daily diet record. It should be kept for at least a week or long enough for you to recognize your individual eating patterns and habits. Everything that you eat and the time of day at which you eat it should be recorded, including meals, snacks, and beverages.

Recording the time of day each time we eat or drink indicates whether we are allowing sufficient time for the body to digest and eliminate food. An irregular eating pattern interrupts the body's natural timing and leads to constipation and digestive disorders. Even if we eat wholesome food, subjecting the body to continuously changing routines may create imbalance and dis-ease. A diet record reveals to us how frequently we eat, what we eat, and whether our diet contains a proper yin-yang balance of pure, wholesome foods. Once a pattern has developed in your diet record, go to a nutritionist to have it analyzed.

One of the major factors that contributes to obesity is malnutrition — an obese person's body is starving for proper nourishment and so the brain is constantly signaling that the body should be fed. A person who does not eat nutritious meals regularly may snack often during the day to appease nagging hunger. Most of us overeat because our diets are not balanced or are incomplete, and psychologically we often feel deprived and unfulfilled. By filling ourselves full, and even beyond, we hope to relieve our lack of ful-fillment. Therefore, to lose weight we should nourish ourselves not only physically but mentally and emotionally as well. That means not criticizing ourselves; the conversations we hold with ourselves should be positive instead of degrading. Replace hope (doubt) with knowing.

We also recommend finding a doctor or other mentor or teacher who understands and practices the science of wholistic health and nutrition. Such a person can help us analyze the causes and effects of our eating habits. The numbers of doctors and experts who are becoming educated in the techniques of wholistic health are increasing dramatically. Today many medical schools, clinics, and health care institutions are emphasizing more strongly than ever before the connection between good health and good nutrition.

There are a few basic guidelines for combining food groups. Although one food at a meal is the most ideal for easy digestion, most people combine several foods at a time. The following chart shows which foods are compatible and, therefore, can provide a well-balanced and complete set of nutrients as well as best digestion.

Some foods are noticeably absent from the chart. They include processed foods, such as white flour and sugar, fried foods, red meat, coffee and alcohol, and what we call artificial foods, made with additives, preservatives, and artificial

FOOD COMBINING FOR EASIEST DIGESTION

One food at a meal is the most ideal for the easiest and best digestion.
Combination of several foods at a meal should be according to the chart below.

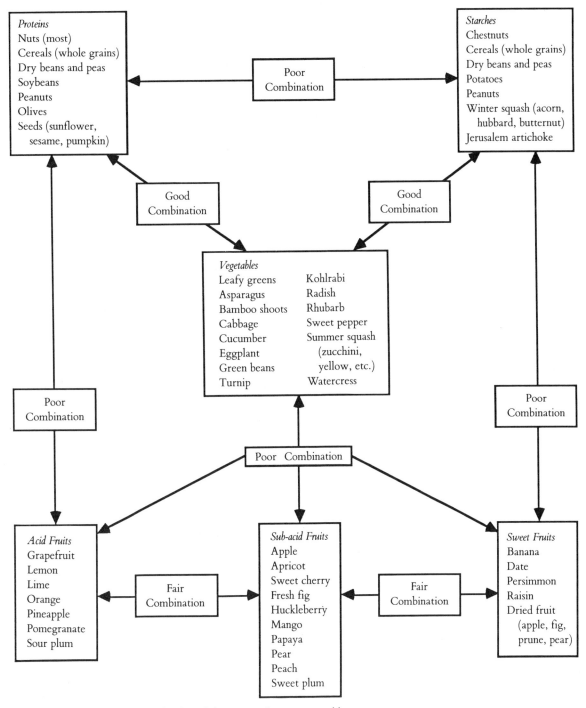

Proteins
Nuts (most)
Cereals (whole grains)
Dry beans and peas
Soybeans
Peanuts
Olives
Seeds (sunflower, sesame, pumpkin)

Starches
Chestnuts
Cereals (whole grains)
Dry beans and peas
Potatoes
Peanuts
Winter squash (acorn, hubbard, butternut)
Jerusalem artichoke

Poor Combination

Good Combination

Good Combination

Vegetables
Leafy greens
Asparagus
Bamboo shoots
Cabbage
Cucumber
Eggplant
Green beans
Turnip
Kohlrabi
Radish
Rhubarb
Sweet pepper
Summer squash (zucchini, yellow, etc.)
Watercress

Poor Combination

Poor Combination

Poor Combination

Acid Fruits
Grapefruit
Lemon
Lime
Orange
Pineapple
Pomegranate
Sour plum

Fair Combination

Sub-acid Fruits
Apple
Apricot
Sweet cherry
Fresh fig
Huckleberry
Mango
Papaya
Pear
Peach
Sweet plum

Fair Combination

Sweet Fruits
Banana
Date
Persimmon
Raisin
Dried fruit (apple, fig, prune, pear)

Avocados are best combined with sub-acid fruits or with green vegetables.
Melons (all kinds) should be eaten alone.

colorings or sprayed with chemicals. These foods contain little, if any, food value. Sugar, artificial flavorings, and chemicals act much like amphetamines, speeding up the body and making us hyper. Red meat is omitted from the chart in part because most livestock is fed chemicals to promote rapid growth. But there are other reasons to avoid red meat as well. In Soviet Georgia, where many people live remarkably long lives, there is a belief that the blood of an animal carries many toxins. On the rare occasions when these villagers eat meat, they boil it to remove the blood of the animal and make a separate vegetable sauce rather than a meat gravy. The Bible, too, prescribes that meat be eaten only in feast or in famine. In some traditions it is believed that an animal releases certain toxins which are caused by fear into its blood stream before it is killed. Hence, meat is not eaten because it is contaminated, so to speak, with these toxins.

In addition to avoiding certain foods, it is best to eat seasonal foods such as fruits and vegetables that are grown locally. We are an intricate part of our local environment. Therefore, foods from other environments with other seasons are "foreign" to us, and the body will not respond to them as well as to home-grown foods.

Another dietary suggestion concerns liquids. Drinks that are too cold go directly to the stomach and interfere with the activity of digestive fluids. We recommend drinks that are warm or at room temperature because they go to the small intestine, where liquids are needed for the body's assimilating and eliminating systems. There is a saying that we should drink our foods and chew our liquids. It means that unless we have chewed our food thoroughly it cannot be properly mixed with saliva. Because the enzymes in saliva prepare the food for the work of the digestive juices, inadequate chewing prevents food from being properly assimilated and eliminated by the body. (See the Suggested Reading List for other, more complete sources of information for individual dietary needs.[1])

Proper nutrition involves not only what we eat but also how we eat. Eating, like all other regularly practiced activities in life, is a ritual. To establish a healthy ritual, we must first eliminate all negative thoughts before eating or preparing a

meal. Ancient wisdom tells us that even the healthies
will become toxic if the mind is toxic. All religious t
recommend an affirmation or prayer before meal pre
and before eating. (e.g., At this time we thank the Di
His/Her offering and commit the energy we receive fr
for the benefit of humankind.) In a similar vein, leftover food
should not be thrown away after a meal; ideally, it should be
given to those who need it. Tons of food that could benefit
others are wasted every day. Eating is one of the ways we
worship the body, which is the temple of the soul; therefore,
the selection, preparation, and eating of food are all forms of
worship.

Daily Mental Nutrition

DAILY MENTAL NUTRITION is as important as daily physical
nutrition. In the section on mental cleansing and balancing in
Chapter 3, we observed that the same techniques that cleanse
the mind also nourish it. Nourishing the mind means
1) avoiding negative thinking, which creates stress and
dis-ease and 2) developing realistic thinking patterns, or "pure
thoughts." Purity of thought is as important in feeding the
mind as purity of food is in feeding the body. Modern
researchers are finding that what we call pure thoughts can
activate adrenalin, hormones, and endorphins, a group of
hormones that act as the body's pain silencers.

Using these two natural mechanisms to nourish the mind
can transform the poisons and toxins created by stress into
positive energy in the body. Life implies growth; growth
requires nourishment; and complete nourishment requires
mental health and balancing.

Endnote
1. For a comprehensive and wholistic overview of the science of nutrition
we recommend *Diet and Nutrition, A Holistic Approach* by Rudolph
Ballentine, M.D. (see Suggested Reading List).

5 RITUALS FOR THE BODY AND MIND

EASTERN PHILOSOPHY AND PSYCHOLOGY teach that the human psyche is veiled with many layers of ignorance that obscure our ability to see the Divine within us. However, at the deepest levels of being, we search for ways to re-establish our connection with the eternal truth, or God. For this reason, according to Eastern wisdom, we take on a human form, or body. Our activities while on earth help us to work through the layers of ignorance, one by one. Finally, after much time and experience, we come to understand the true meaning of Self. In the moment of self-realization the ego is made free — free from the weight of all its illusions and free to reach its eternal destiny, or home.

In this context, the body is a temple and also an instrument that allows us to experience life. A musician regularly tunes his instrument to improve its performance, cleaning and preparing it in a series of movements that look to us like little rituals. Similarly, taking care of the body is a ritualistic tuning by which we grow and perfect ourselves.

Physical Exercise

To MAINTAIN GOOD HEALTH and a youthful appearance we need to establish a system of routine physical exercise. But regular exercise can do more than tone muscles. When practiced with a devotional attitude as a form of worship, physical activity keeps us in tune with life's purpose. In earlier chapters we discussed the word worship as it applies to our mental and physical bodies. Worship means devotion to something we love, admire, and respect. By exercising the body we show respect for the physical instrument that houses the spirit or soul.

We should never begin a routine of physical exercise because we want to be superior to others in strength or beauty. Sometimes, the more we become accomplished in life's activities, the more our ego is inflated. We see ourselves as masterful and, therefore, better than others. There are two motivations for any activity in life, from beginning an exercise routine to opening a business: we can improve ourselves at the expense of others and obstruct our own growth; or we can improve our surroundings, help others to improve and, thereby, expand ourselves. As we develop more physical and mental balance and strength, we participate more fully in creating healthier societies and environments and, finally, a healthier planet.

There are many types of physical exercise and many books, coaches, health clubs, clinics, and other sources for learning and practicing them. Walking is one of the most beneficial forms of gentle exercise, and we recommend a brisk walk twice daily as one method for keeping fit. While walking, as with all forms of physical exercise, it is important to breathe diaphragmatically and through the nose rather than through the mouth. The sinuses, which remove impurities and condition the temperature of air, are one of the body's most sophisticated filtering systems. By breathing through the mouth we 1) by-pass this important protective system and 2) begin to breathe with the chest, which prevents deep, rhythmic breathing and, therefore, wastes energy. As all amateur and professional athletes know, whenever breath control is lost the body and mind become strained, and more susceptible to fatigue and physical injury. By contrast, diaphragmatic breathing through the nose conserves energy and helps develop our stamina and concentration. (See Breath Cleansing Exercises, Chapter 3.)

Of all forms of movement, yoga exercise ranks at the top of our list, because its purpose is to create balance in the body and the mind. Unfortunately, some people associate yoga with mystical religions and cults. This misinterpretation of the science and philosophy of yoga has discouraged many seekers of health and beauty who might otherwise benefit from these invigorating exercises. Although we also recommend other popular forms of physical exercise, such as individual and team sports and aerobics, we have found no other system that is as comprehensive and contributes as much to body-mind wellness as yoga.

The word *yoga* means union. All exercises in yoga, both physical and mental, are designed to unite the body with the mind and the individual self with the Self of all. Yoga has been practiced for centuries, and it plays a major role in the prevention of aging and dis-ease in the ancient tradition of Ayurveda. (See discussion of Ayurveda in Chapter 2.) Yoga is an all-encompassing, or wholistic, science of wellness. Of the many branches or schools in the yoga tradition, we will describe only a few. One branch involves mental practices (Japa Yoga) in which the mind learns to experience reality by focusing on the here and now. Another school teaches physical exercises (Hatha Yoga) that tone and balance the muscles, breath, and nervous system. Yet another school views yoga as a form of worship or a ritual (Karma Yoga) in which all activities are performed selflessly for the benefit of others. All of these branches are separate yet interdependent aspects of a healthy approach to life. Raja Yoga includes all the yogas.

The physical exercises in yoga balance, stretch, tone, and strengthen the body in such a way that the nervous system and the mind can also be balanced and strengthened. Yoga exercises are based upon the premise that our mental and physical bodies work in synergy and that wherever there is synergistic harmony, there is health. In yoga there is no winning or losing and no competition with self or others.

Instead, all of our physical and mental activities become means to achieving the ultimate goal in life, or the realization of self.

Health is not the mere absence of dis-ease in the yoga tradition but rather a dynamic equilibrium of body, breath, mind, and spirit. As we have said, there are many branches of yoga. *Hatha* yoga, which we will discuss in detail, combines poses or postures with deep breathing and relaxation, offering a totally different concept of physical fitness. The aim of yoga exercises is to help the body function optimally, which, in turn, frees the mind and promotes creativity.

Yoga uses slow, thoughtful stretches to enter, hold, and leave each posture. There is a posture for every muscle and joint in the body. The poses activate and stimulate the cardiovascular, digestive, nervous, and endocrine systems. They develop a poised and balanced physique, which is strong and flexible without being muscle-bound.

Yoga can be modified and adapted to suit the needs of everyone, regardless of age or state of health, and its postures provide a challenge to even the most fit. Yoga differs from more conventional exercise in that it emphasizes symmetry and balanced alignment of the musculoskeletal system, especially the full extension of the spinal column. Many sports and exercise regimens involve the repetitive and coordinated contraction of muscles or muscle groups, usually within a specific and limited range of motion. Certain muscle groups, organs, or joints may be ignored, and muscles that are persistently worked without stretching can become hard and tight. These hard, tight muscles misalign the body, inhibiting free movement of the joints and spine, causing general discomfort and inefficient movement, and increasing the chance of injury. Yoga postures, on the other hand, flow from the axis of an extended spine, with the balanced effort of the limbs extending from the spine. By maintaining full spinal extension, space is created for the inter-vertebral discs and spinal nerves, compression of the lower back is relieved, and the abdominal muscles and organs can maintain their tone and function. Once the diaphragm, chest, and lungs are given room to expand, the breath becomes free and gentle, and the mind becomes calm.

There are many yoga postures, but the short series that follows provides a basic well-rounded practice that can be done in twenty to thirty minutes. Please note carefully the following hints and cautions before beginning to practice:

1. If you are under the care of an M.D. or chiropractor, discuss your intention to practice yoga with her or him.

2. Empty the bladder and bowels before practicing. The postures themselves will aid in developing regular bowel movements.

3. Practice in a clean, quiet spot, at a time of day that allows you to be relaxed and quietly attentive to your movements.

4. Wait at least three to four hours after a heavy meal before practicing.

5. Wear comfortable clothing that will allow free movement. Shorts and a T-shirt or a footless leotard work well. Cotton is preferable as it allows the body to breathe. Always practice barefoot.

6. Breathe gently and quietly through the nose. Smooth breathing is more important than deep breathing. Make all movements on the exhalation, and never hold the breath.

7. Keep the eyes and mind quietly attentive to check alignment and make adjustments.

8. Do not bounce into a stretch! Attempting to lengthen a muscle by bouncing or jerking activates the dynamic stretch reflex, which is the mechanism built into the muscle spindles to prevent overstretching and injury. Bouncing actually tightens the muscle and negates the desired effect of stretching.

9. Eliminate extra effort. Work only the muscles necessary to hold the pose; notice and relax any tension in the eyes, face, tongue, jaw, neck, throat, shoulders, and abdomen.

10. If you feel an uncontrollable pain, slowly leave the pose. Examine and adjust the pose to lessen the stretch

and check your alignment. If the pain persists, seek the advice of an experienced teacher.

11. Be persistent and energetic, but at the same time be gentle and nonviolent.

Mountain Pose

TECHNIQUE

Stand erect with the feet together, big toes touching. Contract the thighs and tighten the kneecaps. Tuck the tailbone under, lift the spine and chest. Soften the stomach, roll the shoulders back and down, arms hanging loose. Keep the chin level, throat and eyes relaxed. Distribute the body weight evenly from the heels to the toes. Breathe softly and smoothly.

BENEFITS

Realigns the body, strengthens and corrects deformities of the legs, opens chest, frees and steadies the breath. Forms foundation for all other poses.

Triangle Pose

TECHNIQUE

Stand with the legs four feet apart, arms extended parallel to the floor. Turn the right foot out ninety degrees, left foot in thirty degrees, right heel in line with the middle of the left foot. Contract the thighs and tighten the kneecaps up. On an exhalation, move the right hip back and extend the trunk out over the right leg. Place right hand on shin, extend left arm straight up, palm facing forward. Keep the knees pulled up. Hold twenty to thirty seconds. Repeat on the left side.

BENEFITS

Tones and strengthens the legs, stretches the hamstrings, opens the chest, elongates the spine.

Hero Pose II

TECHNIQUE
Stand with the legs four feet apart, arms extended parallel to
the floor. Turn the right foot out ninety degrees, left foot in
thirty degrees, right heel in line with the middle of the left
foot. Upper body maintains mountain pose. Inhale, tuck
the tail firmly; exhale and bend the right knee to form a
right angle, keeping the left leg straight and firm. The right
knee should be in line with the right hip, directly over the
right heel, shin perpendicular to the floor. Stretch the arms
evenly, keeping the trunk centered over the hips. Hold
twenty to thirty seconds. Repeat on the left side.

BENEFITS
Develops stamina, strengthens ankles, knees, thighs.
Stretches groin, elongates spine, opens chest, strengthens
arms and back.

Extended Side Angle Pose

TECHNIQUE

Stand with the legs four feet apart, arms extended parallel to
the floor. Turn the right foot out ninety degrees, left foot in
thirty degrees, right heel in line with the middle of the left
foot. Inhale, tuck the tail, exhale, and bend the right knee to
form a right angle. Pause. Rest your left hand on your left
hip. Extend the right arm out over the thigh and place the
hand outside the right foot. Stretch the left arm out over the
left ear, palm facing the floor. Hold twenty to thirty
seconds. Repeat to the left.

BENEFITS

Strengthens and tones legs. Reduces fat around waist and
hips, elongates and stretches the spine, opens the chest.
Increases peristaltic activity, aids elimination.

Camel Pose

TECHNIQUE

Kneel on the mat with the knees and feet in line with the hips. Contract the buttocks, arch the back, and place the hands on your heels. Keep the pelvis pushed forward, hips over knees. Turn your toes under if the distance is too great. Drop the head back gently, keeping the neck and throat relaxed. Draw the shoulders away from the ears. Hold ten seconds, build to thirty seconds.

BENEFITS

The whole spine is stretched and toned. Excellent for people with rounded shoulders.

Caution: People with neck problems should not do this pose without a teacher. *There should be no back pain.* If you cannot adjust the stretch to alleviate back pain, consult a teacher.

Spinal Twist

TECHNIQUE

Sit erect on the floor with the legs straight in front. Bend
the right knee and place the right foot on the floor outside
the left knee. Bend the left knee and bring the left foot
outside the right hip. Turn to the right and place the left
arm as close to the shoulder as possible outside the right
knee. Place the right hand on the floor as close to the back
as possible, keeping the back erect. Extend the left arm and
grasp the right foot with the left hand. Turn from the lower
abdomen and waist, lengthening the spine upward as you
turn. Hold twenty to thirty seconds. Repeat to the left.

BENEFITS

Tones and massages abdominal organs. Relieves back pain.
Frees the movement of the shoulders.

Bound Angle

TECHNIQUE

Sit erect on the floor with the legs stretched straight in front. Bend the knees and join the soles of the feet, bringing the heels close to the groin and keeping the spine long. Wrap hands around toes, with little toes on floor. Tilt pelvis forward, descend groin, relax inner thighs. If back rounds and/or knees are higher than hips, sit on a bolster high enough to drop the knees to hip level with the back straight. Hold thirty seconds, build to two to three minutes.

BENEFITS

Stretches inner legs, increases mobility of hips, knees, and ankles. Excellent for maintaining the overall health of the pelvic organs. Together with the shoulder stand, this pose regularizes menstrual periods and helps the ovaries to function properly.

Full Sitting Forward Bend

TECHNIQUE

Sit erect on the floor with the legs stretched straight in front. Extend the heels, contract the thighs, and tighten the knee caps. On an exhalation, roll the pelvis forward, lift and extend the trunk out over the legs. Grasp the calves, ankles, or feet, keeping the chest open. Hold thirty seconds, build to five minutes. If you are stiff, sit on a rolled blanket, loop a belt around the feet and sit erect.

BENEFITS

Stretches legs, strengthens thighs and back, stimulates and tones abdominal organs, massages the heart. Brings blood to the pelvic organs, helps to relieve impotency, and aids in control of ejaculation.

Plough Pose

TECHNIQUE

Lie on a thick blanket that elevates the shoulders and neck
an inch off the floor, shoulders near the edge, neck and head
off the blanket; there should be a space between the neck
and floor. Keep feet and knees together, exhale and bend
the knees to the chest, then roll up onto the shoulders. Bend
the elbows and support the back with the hands. Straighten
the legs, bringing the toes to the floor over head. Contract
the thighs, tighten up the kneecaps, and extend the heels.
Lift the hips, bring the spine into the body and extend up. If
back rounds, place feet up on a chair or wall. Do not push
the chin to the chest. Hold thirty seconds, build to three
minutes.

BENEFITS

Stretches the legs, strengthens the back. Brings flexibility to
the shoulder girdle. Increases blood circulation to the neck
and throat, stimulates thyroid and parathyroid glands.

Cautions: This pose should not be practiced by menstruat-
ing women. Also, people with neck problems should
attempt this pose only under the guidance of an experienced
teacher.

Shoulderstand

TECHNIQUE

As instructed in the plough pose, keep the feet, knees, and thighs together while bending the knees to the chest. Roll the thighs up and extend the legs straight up to the ceiling. Tuck the tail and contract the thighs, extending the legs and back straight up. Hold twenty to thirty seconds, build to three to five minutes.

BENEFITS

Builds endurance, strengthens back, increases venous return to the heart, stimulates endocrine system, relieves fatigue.

Cautions: Do not practice during menstruation. People with neck problems or high blood pressure should attempt this pose only under the guidance of an experienced teacher.

Headstand

TECHNIQUE

Place a folded blanket on the floor and kneel near it. Closely interlock the fingers and rest the forearms on the blanket, elbows no wider than the shoulders. Place the crown of the head on the blanket so that the back of the head touches the palms which are cupped. After securing the head position, raise the knees from the floor, straighten the legs and walk the toes closer to the head. Exhale and gently lift the legs off the floor with the knees bent. Try to swing both feet off the floor simultaneously. Roll the thighs up and straighten the legs. Lift the shoulders, tuck the tail, contract the thighs. Keep the thighs, knees, and big toes touching. Do the pose against a wall if your balance is unsteady. Hold thirty seconds, build gradually to three to five minutes.

BENEFITS

Stimulates the entire organism, creates equilibrium, increases flow of blood to the brain.

Cautions: Ideally, the headstand should be learned under the guidance of an experienced teacher. Also, you should become comfortable in the shoulderstand and understand its dynamics before attempting the headstand. Do not practice any inverted poses during menstruation. Do not practice the headstand if you have high blood pressure, detached retina, glaucoma, obesity, heart problems or stroke, osteoporosis, epilepsy, seizures or other brain disorders, chronic neck problems or whiplash, or conditions requiring aspirin therapy.

Stomach Lift

TECHNIQUE

Stand with the feet in line with the hips, knees slightly bent, hands resting on the thighs. Drop the chin toward the hollow of the throat. Exhale forcefully all the air in your lungs. Holding the breath out, pull the abdominal organs toward the spine and pull the diaphragm up, pressing the hands on the thighs. Hold for four to five seconds. Relax the abdomen, inhale slowly and smoothly. There should be no gasping. Keep the chin to the throat while relaxing the abdomen so as not to strain the heart. Take a few breaths, then repeat.

BENEFITS

Exercises and tones diaphragm and abdominal organs. Increases stomach energy, aids digestion and elimination.

Cautions: Do not practice if you have high blood pressure or heart problems. Practice on an empty stomach after evacuating the bladder and bowels; first thing in the morning is best.

Solar Salutation

The solar salutation, or sun salute, is a series of smooth movements between the poses just described while, at the same time, coordinating the breath. Before practicing the sun salute practice each pose separately, familiarizing yourself with the correct position of each. It is an excellent warm-up before any physical activity, almost a mini-yoga practice in itself, as it includes forward bends, backward bends, groin stretches, and upper body strengtheners.

TECHNIQUE

1. Assume the mountain pose; stand erect and aligned; breathe evenly.
2. Exhale and join the palms together at the center of the chest.
3. Inhale and stretch the arms over the head.
4. Exhale as you extend forward and down into a full forward bend. Hold for two breaths.
5. Exhale as you bend the left knee to a right angle and stretch the right leg straight back, toes turned under. Knee may rest on floor if groin and/or hips are tight. Hold for two breaths.

6. Exhale and stretch the left leg straight back, feet in line with hips, plams flat on floor. Bend the elbows in close to the sides of the chest, lower the body and hold an inch off the floor, keeping the legs straight and the tail tucked. Do not arch the back. Hold for two breaths.

7. With an exhalation, press the floor, arch the back, and lift the chest up between the arms. Stay on your toes, keeping the thighs firmly contracted and the tail bone tucked. Hold for two breaths.

8. Exhale, lift the hips and stretch the legs back, bringing the head between the upper arms forming an upside down V. Stretch the spine up and the heels to the floor. Hold for two breaths.

9. Exhale and swing the right leg forward between the hands. Keep the left leg straight back. Right knee should be over the heel, shin perpendicular to the floor. Hold for two breaths.

10. Exhale, straighten the right leg and bring the left foot next to the right to a bent over, standing position. Knees firm, hips lifting, spine stretching down. Hold for two breaths.

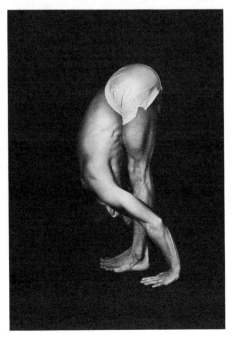

11. Exhale and stretch the arms forward and up extending the arms over the head.

12. Exhale as you join the palms in the center of the chest. Hold for two breaths. This completes one cycle of the solar salutation. Repeat the entire cycle three to six times. After the last cycle, lower the arms to the sides and align the body in the mountain pose. Remain in that pose until the breath has returned to normal.

BENEFITS

Brings flexibility to the spine and legs, stretches the chest, strengthens the arms, warms up the entire body.

Bathing   THROUGHOUT HISTORY, BATHING has been used in rituals and celebrations of self-purification as, for example, in baptisms and birthing. In ancient times bathing was also a highly developed beautifying and rejuvenating practice. Cleopatra bathed in cow's milk and mountain waters containing the essences of herbs and flowers to enhance her renowned beauty.

Men and women today should manage their time so that the ritual of bathing can be enjoyed twice daily, after arising and before retiring for bed. The effects of bathing are not just physical but also mental. Washing the body has the added benefit of making us feel cleaner and fresher mentally as well. We can choose the physical and mental environment that will be most healthy for us at the moment by adding pure, distilled essences from flowers, herbs, and minerals to the bath. Water is one of nature's most relaxing and beautifying elements, and these distilled essences can enhance water's rejuvenating effects. For example, those who suffer from hypertension, stiffness, fatigue, stress, and occasional muscle pain, can benefit by bathing in warm water and aromatic oils. Bathing parts of the body that are especially tense or fatigued, such as the feet, can restore comfort to the entire body and to the mind. Prior to bathing, carefully selected oils can be massaged into areas of tension. Muscles and tissues that are swollen or inflamed can be relieved by bathing in oils that have relaxing and cooling (yin) properties. Essences with a yin effect help us to unwind. By contrast, we can use bath oils with a stimulating or warming (yang) effect to create a feeling of increased energy, which prepares us for any activity. We can even influence our response to the environment by using cooling (yin) oils in summer and warming (yang) oils in winter. This we call "environmental control." The oils used in Aromatherapy (see Chapter 2) can be used singly, but for bathing purposes, they are usually used in combinations. Creating these mixtures is both an art and a science because it involves combining the right oils in the right amounts to produce the desired effect.

To derive maximum benefit from a bath in aromatic waters, we recommend taking time during bathing to practice the exercises described in Chapter 3 for diaphragmatic breathing, self affirmation, kinesthetic and eidetic training, and positive thinking.

The following is a list of a few of the essences derived from trees, flowers, citrus fruits, and spices that are especially appropriate for the bath. We have categorized them according to their stimulating or relaxing properties. (See detailed description of essences in Chapter 2.)

Stimulating and Warming	*Relaxing and Cooling*
TREES	
Cedarwood	Eucalyptus
Frankincense	Siberian Fir
Myrrh	Cypress
Sandalwood	Camphor
FLOWERS	
Lavendar	Rose
Jasmine	Camomile
Neroli (orange blossom)	Ylang Ylang (geranium)
CITRUS FRUITS	
Bergamot	Lemon
	Petitgrain (leave and young roots of Bitter Orange)
	Mandarin
SPICES	
Peppermint	
Marjoram	
Fennel	
Basil	
Wintergreen	

We advise using all essences of spices with caution — one or two drops is sufficient — because they tend to have a stimulating and warming effect on the skin. If used in excess they will have a temporary stinging effect and may cause skin irritation. Herbal essences and distilled oils from flowers can be combined with natural detergents to make excellent foaming bath formulas. Some herbal essences can be obtained, for example, at health food stores and through reputable distributors and pharmaceutical houses. We recommend dealing always with experts in the field of Aromatherapy to obtain herbal preparations with maximum purity and potency.

Oral hygiene is associated with the twice-daily bathing practice. Herbal essences used in Aromatherapy, such as peppermint, fennel, and cinnamon, to name only a few, have long been used in oral hygiene products. Today there are many toothpastes, mouthwashes, and even dental flosses made with natural ingredients and flavorings, and we encourage using them exclusively. The teeth and gums can be kept strong and healthy for many years with a good diet and a daily routine of thorough brushing and flossing to prevent decay and gum infections. It is also helpful to use a tongue scraper or a spoon to remove any toxic materials coating the tongue, which may be caused by poor digestion. Other activities that cleanse and beautify the body should also accompany bathing. For example, relaxing in aromatic waters is the perfect time for men and women to apply facial masques, shave, and attend to all their cleansing needs.

Skin Care

THE FACE IS A LANDSCAPE of our inner thoughts and feelings. The law of cause and effect paints on the face a picture of the path in life that we have followed. Depression, worry, and anxiety become part of the facial expression of those who are unhappy, just as optimism and joy are reflected on the faces of those who remain youthful looking throughout life.

In traditional Oriental medicine, the face is an indicator of health or dis-ease. By studying skin colorations and the condition of the face, we can determine the condition of the internal organs. Figure 5.1 shows which facial areas are linked to specific organs; and the following description is a brief diagnostic guide:

Intestines — the forehead area. Breakouts in this area may be an indication that the colon is congested or that purging and cleansing is occurring. If the area is red, we may be eating salt,

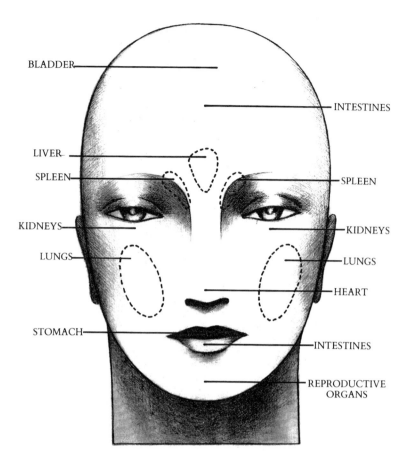

BLADDER

INTESTINES

LIVER

SPLEEN

SPLEEN

KIDNEYS

KIDNEYS

LUNGS

LUNGS

HEART

STOMACH

INTESTINES

REPRODUCTIVE
ORGANS

red meats, or dairy products (yang foods) in excess. If the area is white, we may be consuming too much sugar, chemicals, drugs, caffeine, or fruit (yin foods). (See Food Chart in Chapter 4.)

The lips. Digestion begins at the lips, and, since the dyes from lipstick may interfere with enzymes in the mouth and the saliva, removing lipstick before eating may help the digestion process. If the lips are dry and cracked, the intestines may not be functioning properly. Eating foods high in preservatives contributes to poor digestion.

Liver — between the eyes. A vertical line here may indicate a temperamental personality or a liver weakness or disorder. Liver malfunctions can be caused from preservatives, alcohol, and drugs (yang foods).

Spleen — either side of the brow bone. Lines here may indicate a weakness in the spleen area. The spleen is another filtering organ which, once clogged with toxins, will create stress-related illnesses and changes in behavioral patterns. Lines here may also be correlated to tightness in the shoulder area, which can be a signal that the adrenal glands are malfunctioning.

Kidneys — area under the eyes. A kidney malfunction may show itself by a darkening under the eyes, either brown or black in color. If the area under the eyes is also puffy and red, we probably use too many rich foods, alcohol, and/or nicotine (extreme yin and yang foods).

Male sexual organs — area surrounding nose. Redness in this area may be a warning of a future malfunction of the prostrate gland. Redness here also suggests that we are eating many foods that are yang extremes; whiteness indicates yin extreme foods.

Heart — the tip of the nose. Redness, expanded capillaries or swollen tissue in this area may indicate high blood pressure and a tendency toward heart conditions.

Lungs — the nostrils and cheek area. If there are blackheads, whiteheads, or irritations in this area, we probably have frequent colds and bronchitis and consume a fair amount of dairy products (which form mucus in the lungs) as well as sugar (a yin extreme food).

Stomach — area surrounding lips. Breakouts in this area may indicate an inability to digest food well, possibly due to an enzyme deficiency in the acid of the stomach.

Female reproductive organs — chin area. Breakouts in this area are usually connected to the mentrual cycle. Areas on the sides of the chin which are white and blotchy, either with congestion or suffocation (a small granular-like feeling under the skin), may indicate a yeast infection. If the chin is always red, swollen, and either suffocated or congested, it may mean that there is some structural weakness of the reproductive organs.

No matter what these signs indicate, we can greatly improve the condition of the skin and body with proper diet, regular exercise, and a program of daily skin care.

DAILY SKIN CARE PROGRAM   Every day our skin is under constant attack from the damaging effects of dirt, dust, pollution, sun, and drying wind. We recommend the following three-step daily skin care program as an effective, convenient way to counteract these effects. If practiced daily, this routine will help the skin remain young and healthy looking.

Step 1: Cleansing

Proper skin treatment begins with the removal of dirt, oily secretions, and debris from the skin. All cleansing products, including creams, foams, and gels, should contain ingredients that have a gently stimulating (yang) effect on the skin. A natural cleanser in an alkaline base can open the pores and enter deep within them to destroy harmful bacteria. In contrast to natural alkaline products, soaps and cleansers with synthetic ingredients are acid-based. Therefore, rather than opening the pores, they tighten the skin and are unable to cleanse the pores deeply and thoroughly.

Some of nature's mildest yet most beneficial cleansers are made from the distilled essences of flowers and forest trees and herbs. For example, the word lavender comes from the Latin *lavare,* which means to wash, and lavender was once one of the most popular cleansing essences. Spice essences are not appropriate ingredients in cleansers because of their warming and overstimulating effects on the skin.

We recommend the following procedure for thoroughly cleansing the skin. Moisten the face with lukewarm water. Place a half teaspoon of natural cleansing cream in the palm and spread the cream evenly over the face and throat. Using the fingertips, gently massage with small rotary movements upwards and outwards, avoiding the delicate eye area. Rinse off with lukewarm water. Pat dry with a natural towel. Repeat this process if you wear heavy makeup.

Step 2: Nourishing

Once the face has been properly cleansed, we can apply a masque especially suited to our skin type and condition. There are two types of masques. Those with a heating effect stimulate the circulation of blood at the surface of the skin, and those with a relaxing and cooling effect contract the pores and blood vessels to retain nourishment and moisture and protect the skin from harmful bacteria. Generally, a masque that contains stimulating (yang) ingredients is applied first, and it is followed by a masque with relaxing (yin) qualities. If there isnot sufficient time for the application of both masques, one immediately following the other, we can apply a stimulating masque in the morning when bathing and preparing for the day and a relaxing masque before retiring for bed.

Step 2 should always include the use of a nourishing skin-care *infusion* suitable for our skin type. These infusions are made from the distilled essences of flowers and herbs, and each infusion is a unique formula of ingredients that stabilizes the skin's condition. For example, the infusion for oily skin is especially designed to restore the skin's balance of natural oils. The art and science of creating these formulas involves properly selecting and combining natural essences and ingredients to balance each skin type.

The skin is now ready to receive the beneficial effects of a natural moisturizer. Moisturizing cream should be used in the morning and evening to nourish the skin. Moisten the face with lukewarm water. Place one-quarter teaspoon of natural moisturizing cream into the palm and smooth the cream evenly over the face and throat. Gently press into the skin, being careful around the eye area. Avoid getting skin-care products in eyes; if eye contact occurs, rinse with water.

Step 3: Toning

After the skin has been cleansed, it should be treated with a natural toner to remove any surface impurities that may remain after cleansing. A toner will help remove these impurities, constrict pores, and prepare the skin for additional moisture. The most effective toners or astringents are made from the pure essences of flowers. Rosewater is an age-old skin toner that is made by soaking rose petals for many days in distilled water or in pure mountain or mineral waters. The rose essence has a relaxing or cooling (yin) effect on the skin. A few drops of other flower essences can be added to the rosewater toner to treat particular skin types and conditions.

The application procedure is simple and leaves the skin feeling refreshed. Tilt the head back and close the eyes. Spray the toner three to five inches from the face, allowing the gentle mist to fall on the facial surface. Press the toner into the face with the fingers until dry.

There are four types of skin: dry, oily, a combination of dry and oily, and normal. The following is a description of and skin care program for each type.

Dry Skin

Dry skin is characterized by a lack of moisture on the skin's surface. The pores on the nose, forehead, and chin are slightly larger, and the oil is usually confined to those areas. Breakouts are generally due to hormonal fluctuations, stress, climate changes, and dietary variations. These skin eruptions appear in the form of whiteheads, which are pores filled with sebum (the body's natural oil). The excess oil trapped in this way cannot escape to the skin's surface. Dry skin is generally thinner than normal skin and is susceptible to expanded capillaries and sensitivities, making skin look red and blotchy.

Dry skin should be cleansed at least once daily with a natural preparation designed to rid the skin's surface of excess sebum without drying the skin. Dry skin needs more stimulation to push the sebum through the pores which are sometimes too small. Because dry skin tends to be more sensitive than normal skin, we should avoid harsh chemicals that may damage or dry the skin even more.

A cleansing scrub is useful once or twice a week to stimulate the skin's secretion of oil and to get rid of dead skin cells. Because of the abrasive action of cleansing scrubs, they should be used with slow and gentle movements. Although some stimulation is recommended for dry skin, too much stimulation can exacerbate symptoms.

Applying a facial masque especially designed for dry skin is an excellent way to stimulate the moisturizing process. Since dry skin tends to lose moisture faster than oily skin, it is important to replenish lost moisture by using a masque that smothers the skin by attracting moisture toward the surface. After moisture has been brought to the surface, it needs to be kept there so that the tissues remain moisturized and plump; moisture reduces the prominence of wrinkles. Another benefit of the masque is the purging action, which rids skin of embedded particles. This step is important for presoftening

and purging before blackheads and whiteheads can be re
moved.

After masquing, rosewater facial toner should be used
help neutralize and draw moisture further into the skin and to
remove any remaining impurities. A moisturizer can be
applied at this stage to seal in the moisture and protect the
skin's surface.

Oily Skin

Oily skin is characterized by larger pores over a majority of
the facial surface, sometimes to the extreme outer edges of the
face. It is smoother in texture, thicker and more pliable than
dry skin because it contains more sebum. Due to its ability to
retain moisture, this type of skin tends to remain youthful
looking longer than dryer skin, and it has more flexibility and
fewer wrinkles.

We associate oily skin with an over-secretion of sebum,
which throws off the acid balance on the surface, creating
blackheads, pustules (blackheads that have broken through the
skin's surface and become infected with strep or staph bacteria
on the skin), and whiteheads. These congregate most heavily
on the areas of the body that have the greatest concentration of
impurities. The condition of oily skin varies greatly as a result
of our efforts to get rid of the excess oil. The extreme situation
occurs when more oil is created on the skin surface due to
over-stimulation by excess washing with abrasive scrubs,
harsh products, or chemicals. This condition can be treated in
a number of ways, but monitoring the diet is essential. The
oilier the skin, the more necessary natural products and good
diet become.

Oily skin can be cleansed twice to three times daily,
depending upon the amount of oil present on the surface.
Over-cleansing should be discouraged because it will only
bring more oil to the skin's surface. A natural cleansing scrub
also may be used once a week to help remove eruptions and to
stimulate the purging of particles directly under the skin's
surface. Again, overuse of a cleansing scrub on oily skin may
create more oil on the skin's surface.

A proper masque is essential for oily skin. The weekly application of a pure, natural product mask with relaxing properties will help purge, cleanse, and moisturize the skin, and will aid in normalizing sebum production. A mask with more stimulating properties will nourish, moisturize, and soften the skin while toning and tightening the tissues. Toning the skin with a pure facial toner helps to maintain a neutralized balance on the skin by bringing it to a pH balance of seven, ridding the surface of any impurities, and prepares the skin to receive moisture.

Oily skin still requires moisture, not oil, to be properly balanced, or protected, sealed, and nourished. If skin is excessively oily, distilled water may be placed on the fingertips before applying moisturizing cream. To remove cream not absorbed by the skin, gently blot off the excess with a tissue.

Combination Skin

This skin type has characteristics of both dry and oily skin. For example, certain areas of the face, such as the chin and forehead, can be especially dry or oily. As we discussed earlier in this chapter, diagnostic procedures in Oriental and Ayur-vedic medicine link the facial areas to specific organs in the body. Therefore, an area of the face that is particularly dry or oily may indicate some imbalance in the corresponding internal organ. Balance can be restored through proper diet, exercise, and use of proper skin care products, described in the previous sections on dry and oily skin types.

Normal Skin

Normal skin is characterized by a small area of enlarged pores on the forehead, nose, and chin areas. This skin type is generally well balanced with few eruptions; these are due mainly to stress, climate changes, hormonal disturbances, or nutritional variances. Coloration is usually even and well balanced, and normal skin typically looks fresh and moist, giving it a healthy glow. Even though this skin type appears to have no apparent problems, with neglect or mistreatment, problems can develop quickly. Proper maintenance with natural skin care products will enhance the beauty that already exists and will create more beauty in the years to come.

A cleansing cream for normal to dry skin can be used twice daily to help rid the skin's surface of excess oil and impurities. In addition, cleansing will stimulate circulation to sluggish areas of built-up sebum, which may appear occasionally as whiteheads or blackheads around the eye, nose, forehead, and chin areas.

A natural cleansing scrub can be used for normal skin once or twice a week, depending upon 1) whether the skin needs to shed dead skin cells and 2) how many expanded capillaries there are on the facial surface. Normal skin is generally more pliable and durable than dry skin, and it can tolerate more stimulation than oily skin. Therefore, it can reap the full benefits of a facial scrub without much possibility of unfavorable results.

A natural facial toner rids the skin of remaining particles, neutralizes the skin's surface, and prepares it to receive moisture. Now the skin is ready to be sealed, nourished, and protected with a moisturizer.

SKIN PRODUCTS   Many skin care products manufactured today contain mineral oil and synthetic fragrances and ingredients. Mineral oil is a petroleum derivative that has long been used in cosmetics because of its good mixing qualities. We believe that body care products are "external foods," which can be absorbed by the skin and hair, and, therefore, should be as pure, natural, and wholesome as the foods we eat. Since gasoline fuel is not a source of food, it seems reasonable that we would not use petroleum-derived products to nourish the face and body.

Collagen is another popular ingredient in today's cosmetics, and manufacturers advertise it as a youth-restoring agent. Collagen is a gelatin-like animal protein which, we believe, has little, if any, relationship to proteins in the human body. Some people have had collagen injected under the flesh to fill out the skin and eliminate wrinkles. It is our opinion that collagen injections may act somewhat like silicone under the skin which, over a period of time, may shift in an uncontrollable manner. We have yet to find conclusive evidence that some of these synthetic products slow down aging; in fact, their artificial properties may actually speed up the aging process. Rather than ingesting and injecting into the body so-called restorative agents, such as hormones and steroids, which may alter the body's chemical balance, we recommend using products that are natural to the body and enhance its own rhythms and rejuvenating processes. For example, one of the best and most natural ways to moisturize the body's tissues is to drink plenty of pure water. Too often, in our rush to keep up with the latest fashion trends, we neglect the age-old principles of health and beauty.

The body is an intricately designed mechanism that recycles itself moment by moment. While we cannot arrest the aging process, we can support the body's rejuvenating systems by eating nutritious foods, exercising regularly, staying mentally well balanced, and using natural body care products. One who ages gracefully enjoys life and sees the aging process as an exciting and purposeful adventure.

THE ART OF FACE PAINTING

Today's styles in makeup are dictated by the international, multi-million dollar fashion and cosmetics industries. These companies set and change the trends in makeup, or face painting, so rapidly that consumers are accustomed to buying new fashion colors every season. Also, in recent years the use of makeup by men is becoming socially acceptable. Men's fashion magazines encourage their male readers to use preparations that correct and protect the skin and to wear natural shades of makeup to harmonize skin tones.

Many of the makeup styles worn by famous models and advertised in high fashion magazines may not be appropriate for most of us. Whether or not men and women wear makeup and the styles they select are matters of personal choice. Nevertheless, following the fashion trends can be a creative expression of our self-image and can help us feel youthful and in step with change. Wearing up-to-date makeup styles can motivate us to think young by maintaining positive psychological attitudes towards ourselves and life. Facial makeovers are popular today because they bring us out of the past and into the present, thereby giving us a fresh, or youthful, perspective on life.

We can get inspiration for makeup changes by studying fashion magazines and by consulting skin care consultants who know the latest fashion trends. The eyes, known as the windows of the soul, are the focal point of a beautiful face. For centuries women have used makeup to bring attention to the eyes because the eyes are expressive tools in the art of communication. We recommend that eye shadow and mascara shades should not duplicate the eye color. Instead, complimentary colors should be used because they accent rather than dilute the color of the iris.

The lips are also important in makeup artistry. In applying lipstick, we suggest that the natural outlines of the mouth be followed, unless the desired effect is to draw particular attention to the lips. There are no hard and fast rules in the art of face painting, for what is "in" today is "out" tomorrow. Nevertheless, good health is never out of fashion, and consumers should insist that all makeup and face care products be made from pure, naturally-derived substances.

SUN BATHING   Limited exposure to the sun is one of the most important parts of any skin care program. However, just as the sun's rays can be nourishing, they can also be devastating when taken in excess. The time of day and the length of time for sun exposure is critical. Never lay in the sun for hours, no matter how healthy and thick the skin or how much protective sun screen is used. It is now an accepted medical fact that most skin cancers are caused from too much sun exposure. The sun's rays during the two hours at high noon are the most damaging; however, ten to twenty minutes of sunning in the early or midmorning or in the middle or late afternoon can be beneficial. Sun bathing in the nude for short periods can be a source of skin nourishment for the entire body. The sun bath is an excellent opportunity for practicing relaxation, breathing, and grounding exercises, which calm the body and the mind. (See Relaxation Section in Chapter 3.)

Massage

THE FLOW OF ENERGY IN THE BODY circulates from lower to upper and from upper to lower regions in a continous cycle. When the body is healthy, this flow is even, constant, and uninterrupted. However, when stress occurs, the body reacts by contracting the muscle tissues, and contracted muscles block the free flow of energy in the body. Then circulation slows down and calcium deposits can form, for example, on the bottoms of the feet and on the insides of the hands. We all know that by not using a camera or tape recorder for a long time the batteries become corroded. Something similar happens to our bodies when nutrients like calcium, which are unable to flow freely through the system, crystalize in specific areas. These crystalizations, or deposits, need to be broken up so that they can re-enter the bloodstream and be discharged through the kidneys. Chronic mental and physical stress causes stiffness, pain, and the inability to flex, stretch, and move muscles easily and comfortably — the most common symptoms of aging.

Massaging is an excellent method for relieving stress and for preventing the accumulation of tension in the body. In western society, massage has often been given a negative, and some-times a sexual, connotation. This is unfortunate because the therapeutic effects of massage are many. The art of massage has been known and practiced for centuries by doctors, nurses, masseuses and masseurs, parents, children, and spouses. Massage, as a technique for achieving and maintaining wellness, belongs in the home as part of our close and loving relationships. The best way to creat closeness in a relationship is to relieve another's tension and to help him or her to feel well. Therefore, massage should be learned by everyone and practiced daily as a health-giving gift to ourselves and others.

There are many helpful books on massaging techniques, but we also recommend taking lessons and classes from competent professionals. Male and female partners should attend massage classes together and practice the techniques on each other. What follows is a brief description of some of the major schools of massage.

ACUPRESSURE MASSAGE Acupressure massage uses the same pressure point system as acupuncture, one of the oldest forms of Oriental medicine. However, acupressure massage does not use the acupuncture technique of inserting needles at certain pressure points in the body. Instead, the middle finger of each hand gently but deeply massages the pressure points.

A healthy, unobstructed energy flow actually can be felt as pulsations emanating from the pressure points into the middle fingers of the person giving the massage. To be sensitive to these pulsations, the massage giver should be in a grounded state and mentally focused on the other's wellness. Throughout an acupressure massage the fingers should press and release and press and release at each pressure point. If no pulsation is felt at a pressure point, massage in a counterclockwise direction. If there is still no pulsation, massage clockwise until pulsation begins. In this manner each pressure point is stimulated so that the energy flow is re-established in the body.

FIGURE 5.2:

Acupuncture meridians and pressure points

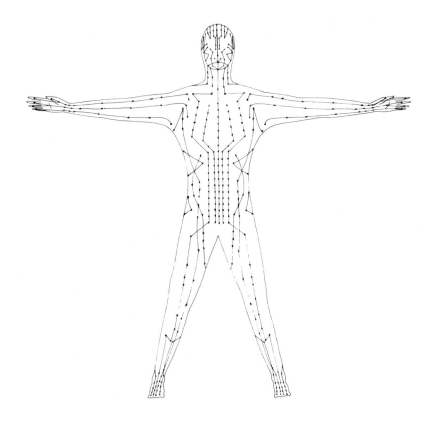

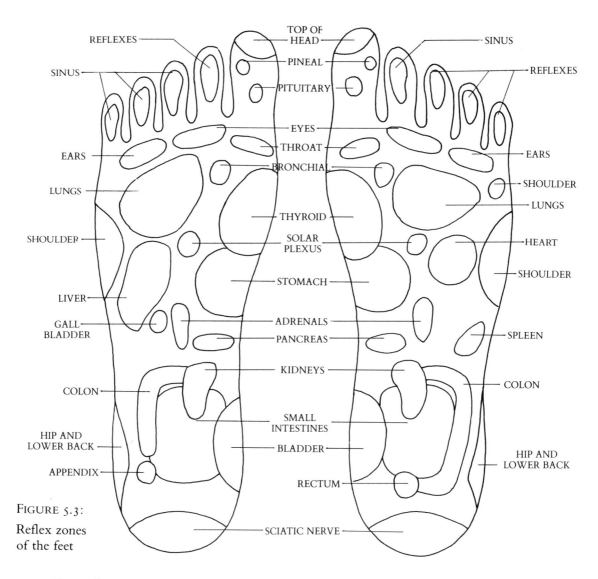

TOP OF HEAD
REFLEXES
SINUS
PINEAL
PITUITARY
SINUS
REFLEXES
EYES
THROAT
BRONCHIAL
EARS
EARS
SHOULDER
LUNGS
LUNGS
THYROID
SHOULDER
SOLAR PLEXUS
HEART
STOMACH
SHOULDER
LIVER
GALL BLADDER
ADRENALS
PANCREAS
SPLEEN
KIDNEYS
COLON
COLON
SMALL INTESTINES
HIP AND LOWER BACK
BLADDER
HIP AND LOWER BACK
APPENDIX
RECTUM
SCIATIC NERVE

FIGURE 5.3:
Reflex zones
of the feet

FOOT REFLEXOLOGY   Just as certain areas of the face indicate imbalances in specific organs, the feet also mirror our inner health. In the foot reflexology diagram (Figure 5.3), the soles of the feet are divided into segments that correspond to organs and glands throughout the body. Therefore, massaging particular areas of the feet stimulates the corresponding organ or gland.

In foot reflexology massage, the thumb or the entire knuckle is used in a deep, rotating motion. The massage giver begins at the heel of the foot, which corresponds to the lower part of the body, and moves up to the toes, which are linked to the head.

SWEDISH MASSAGE Swedish massage is a whole-body massage technique in which the entire hand is used to stimulate the back, trunk, and limbs. This type of massaging always moves toward the heart — a massage beginning at the feet or the hands moves up toward the heart area, and a massage beginning at the head moves down toward the heart. The massage giver should remain sensitive to the other's comfort throughout the massage. Areas of tension should be worked on deeply but without causing pain. Some people give massages that are extraordinarily painful, but we believe that painful massages actually create more tension and stress. Only when the body is thoroughly relaxed can tension be released.

FACIAL MASSAGE An important revitalizing practice frequently neglected today is the facial massage. By following the sixteen steps described and pictured here, we can stimulate and exercise facial muscles and tissues in a few minutes time.

1. With the middle and ring fingers, rotate gently in a figure eight pattern applying pressure on the upward movement to the temple pressure point. Repeat three to five times.

2. Begin a circular movement with the middle finger at the outside corner of the eye, continue on the cheek bone to a point under the center of the eye, then slide the finger to the pressure point above the inside corner of the eye.

3. Apply gentle pressure to the sinus pressure point, letting the other fingers drop on the brow and slide back to the starting point, and repeat. Do steps one through three as one continuous movement.

4. Without stopping the continuous movement, move to the outside corner of the eye and lift in an upward rolling movement using the middle and ring fingers.

5. Continue the rolling movement across the forehead.

6. Continue the rolling movement on the right side, repeat back and forth across the forehead.

7. With the same nonstop motion, continue the rolling movement from the cheeks down to the jaw. Continue moving upward gently, lifting the cheek muscles.

8. With the index finger above the chin and jawline and the little fingers below, slide across the chin and continue the rolling movement on the right cheek. Continue back and forth three to five times.

9. Using the first three fingers, roll one finger following the other as each finger lifts the corner of the mouth. Repeat on each side of the mouth.

10. Now the index finger and middle finger "scissor" from the center of the face up and out toward the ear lobes. The left hand is on the left side of the face and the right hand is on the right side.

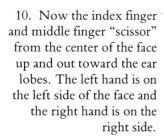

11. Beginning at the corners of the mouth, work in a rotary movement towards the center of the lower lip and back to the corners of the mouth. Repeat five times.

12. Work from the center of the upper lip to the outside corner of the lip and up the sides of the nose with the same rotary movement. Repeat three to five times.

13. With the hands alternating one over the other, gently but firmly slide them from underneath the chin, ending when the fingers reach the upper cheek bone. Then, still alternating, the hands should start on the forehead and slide to the temple area in the opposite direction. Rotate this motion back and forth.

14. Beginning in the center of the forehead, work one side at a time, dividing the forehead horizontally into three parts. Rotate the muscle with the thumb working toward the temple pressure point, press and release. Repeat on the other side.

15. Beginning in the center of the forehead, work one half at a time. Using the thumb, rotate, moving the forehead muscle to the temple pressure point. Press gently and release.

16. To end the massage, hand pressure should go from firm to very light until the hands are gradually feathered off the forehead; or gently cover the eyes with both hands and lightly feather off.

Facial Exercises

Facial exercises should be practiced daily on an empty stomach using the diaphragmatic breathing technique described in Chapter 3. For each exercise, contract the muscles to full capacity on exhalation and sustain the contraction as long as possible. Relax the contracted muscles on inhalation and repeat the exercise again. Each exercise should be repeated three times.

THE FACIAL SQUINT:
Contract every muscle in the face to full capacity and hold as long as possible. Relax on inhalation.

BENEFITS:
Blood flow to face and neck is increased nourishing the facial tissue. The facial muscles are toned and relaxed, reducing and preventing winkles. Tension is released.

MOUTH EXERCISE:
Grin to maximum capacity on exhalation and hold. Relax on inhalation.

BENEFITS:
Releases tension in facial muscles and tones facial tissue and muscles. Reduces and helps prevent wrinkles.

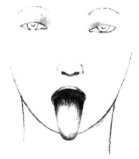

THE LION:
Stretch the tongue out and down as far as possible on exhalation and hold. Relax on inhalation.

BENEFITS:
Excellent for throat problems, releases tension in throat and is helpful with throat infections. Do this exercise after gargling with salt water infused with peppermint, anise, or basil.

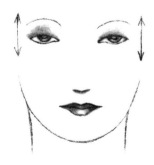

Eye Exercises
As in the facial exercises, the eye exercises use diaphragmatic breathing. Each exercise should stretch the eye muscles to their full capacity and be held as long as possible. Contract muscles on exhalation, relax on inhalation. Repeat exercises three times.

UP AND DOWN EYE MOVEMENTS:
Look up on exhalation and hold; relax on inhalation. Look down on exhalation and hold; relax on inhalation.

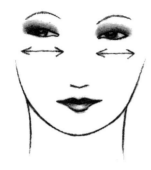

LEFT TO RIGHT EYE EXERCISES:
Look to the extreme left on exhalation and hold; relax on inhalation. Look to the extreme right on exhalation and hold; relax on inhalation.

DIAGONAL EYE EXERCISES:
Move the eye from the extreme upper left corner to the extreme lower right corner on exhalation and hold; relax on inhalation. Move the eye from the extreme upper right corner to the extreme lower left corner on exhalation and hold; relax on inhalation.

ROTATING EYE EXERCISE:
Circle the eyes to the left on exhalation; rest on inhalation. Circle the eyes to the right on exhalation; rest on inhalation.

BENEFITS:
Helpful in strengthening the eye muslces and preventing the weakening of eyesight.

This massage has been developed to promote the drainage of
the body's excess fluids and impurities. Before beginning the
step-by-step massage outlined below, pre-cleanse the skin
using a skin product best suited to your skin type, and apply a
lubricating infusion directly to the face, shoulders, and chest
area.[1]

1. The Facial Clearing Step

The Facial Clearing Step will rejuvenate and increase the
health of the skin by flushing and clearing the fluids and
impurities that are trapped within the skin tissue. After each
phase of the Facial Clearing Step, follow with a stroking
motion down the front of the neck.

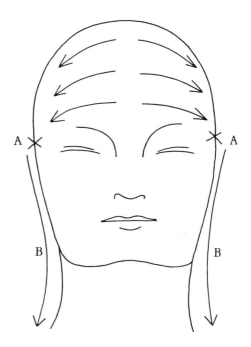

Place the middle finger of each hand on the mid-line of the
forehead at eyebrow level. Draw fingers out to points A and
then to points B. Repeat this process working up the entire
forehead.

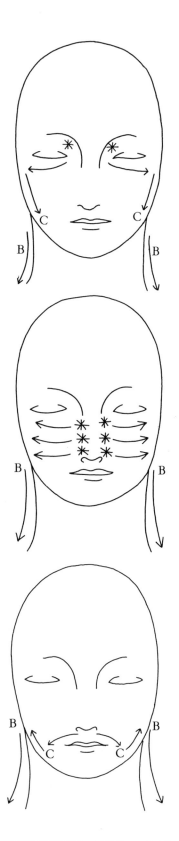

Carefully place fingers at the point where the nose meets the eyes and apply moderate pressure for five seconds (being careful not to allow fingers or infusion to come in contact with the eyes). Draw the fingers out and down to points C and then to points B.

Place fingers on either side of the nose (where the nostrils meet the face), and apply pressure for five seconds. Draw fingers out to points B. Repeat this process, working up along the sides of the nose to where the nose meets the eyes.

Place your fingers directly below the nose; using a gentle rotating movement draw out to points C, then out to points B.

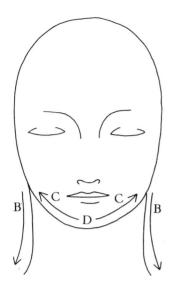

Begin directly below the mouth at point D, gently massaging the chin area; draw the fingers to points C, then out to points B.

2. The Elimination Step

The Elimination Step clears the front and back neck area, allowing the proper channeling of impurities from the facial area.

At point E, gently place fingers of both hands on the center of the throat and draw impurities to the sides. Placing fingers slightly higher with each stroke, work up to points B on either side of the neck.

From points B, draw fingers back along the base of the skull to the center point behind the head. Using gentle, circular movements, massage back out to points B.

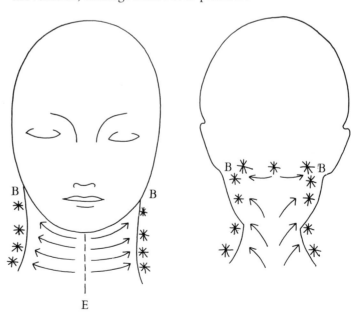

From points B, work down to point E using the lower part of the thumbs and palms to make downward, circular movements. Follow with a flushing stroke from points B to point E.

(Repeat this step 3 times.)

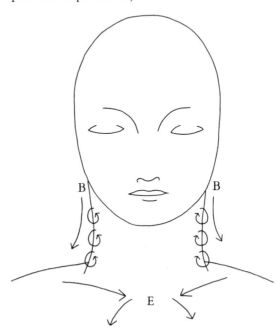

3. The Rejuvenating Breast Massage

Because of the concentration of fatty tissue in the breast region, congestion in the normal flow of circulation may occur, inhibiting the proper release of fluids and impurities. For this reason, it is beneficial to perform the Rejuvenating Breast Massage.

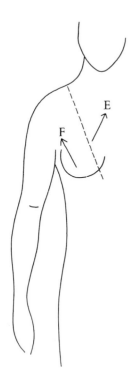

Begin with the outer right breast region; use short, drawing strokes, drawing inpurities up to point F.

For the inner breast area, draw impurities up to point E.

(Repeat these steps on the left breast.)

Note: The Rejuvenating Breast Massage is not recommended for pregnant or nursing women.

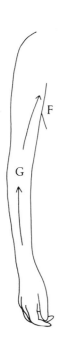

4. The Clearing Step

This step will allow the proper passage of impurities from the arm and chest areas.

Begin at the mid-upper right arm, using smooth strokes to gently pass impurities up toward point F. Gently press point F to improve the passage of fluids. Repeat this step, beginning slightly lower each time, to the fold of the elbow.

Beginning at the mid-lower arm, draw impurities up to point G and then up to point F. Repeat this process, beginning slightly lower each time until you reach the wrist.

(Repeat these steps on the left arm.)

Hair Care

HAIRSTYLES, MAKEUP, AND DRESS are accessories for the body. Usually we see them as ways to highlight our best features and to hide our less favorite ones. However, by experimenting creatively with these accessories, we will discover that what we thought of as facial or body flaws can become the most striking and uniquely beautiful aspects of our appearance.

Fashion magazines today are an excellent source of the latest hairstyles, fashions, and makeup techniques. They serve as consumer guides, and we recommend studying them carefully before undertaking a major change in appearance. Fashion editors are better informed than most hairdressers because they follow the trends set by internationally famous beauty experts. It is best to go to a beauty salon having done some research and with a hairstyle in mind and a clear idea of the self-image we want to project.

A master hair stylist is a skilled artist who can recognize a client's inner beauty and bring it to the surface. Selecting a stylist who interprets beauty as we do requires research; and so we should investigate a stylist's work, just as we would investigate the background of any other person before entering into a new relationship. Most of us are psychologically attached to our appearance, and hair is an important part of this self-image. Altering our appearance either gives us a new appreciation of our beauty or disappoints us. In other words, we all know exactly what we want after the fact! To prevent disappointment with a new hairstyle we should communicate clearly, making sure that the stylist understands our expectations and interprets our business and personal image as we do. A master stylist's work is usually well worth the price. However, when hairstyling is expensive, it is even more important to do thorough research and communicate well with the stylist, for we stand to lose both psychologically and financially. In addition to inquiring about a stylist's professional reputation, we recommend observing the stylist at work. In this way we can see how clients are treated and whether they are satisfied with the results.

Once we have found a suitable hairstyle, we should begin a regular program of hair care. Hair, like the skin, needs three ingredients to look healthy: 1) moisture (water), 2) lubrication (natural oils), 3) formulas with natural ingredients to correct imbalances and remove impurities.

All daily hair maintenance programs involve shampooing and conditioning, but there are no rules for how often we need to shampoo and condition the hair. For example, to maintain a fluffy, full style, we may want to shampoo and condition every day. The quality of the products we use is more important than how often we use them. Most shampoos sold today in beauty salons and drug and department stores contain about 50 percent water and about 45 percent synthetically-derived detergent. Synthetic detergents are creamy and create large quantities of lather, but, we believe, they tend to dry the hair and scalp. There are high quality natural detergents, such as coconut, wheat germ, and olive oil, which not only cleanse but also nourish the hair and scalp.

The remaining ingredients in most modern shampoos are synthetic fragrances, emulsifying agents, and wax-like plastic-derived polymers designed to manage the hair. While the fragrance and creaminess may have pleasant psychological effects, these plastic-derived polymers cling to and coat the hair. The gradual build up of synthetic chemicals on the hair and scalp prevents hydration, the process by which moisture enters and leaves the hair shaft. When the hair is coated with synthetic chemicals it becomes limp and dry.

Some manufacturers include animal protein in their hair care products. Because hair is made of protein, consumers believe that these products nourish the hair; but the external application of animal protein is of no use in hair growth and adds yet another filmy coating on the hair. Some beauty experts recommend changing brands of shampoos every three to four months to prevent the build-up of synthetic chemicals, but most shampoos today contain basically the same ingredients. The only substantive differences are in name, fragrance, packaging, and promotional literature.

Conditioners, hair styling gels, mousses and temporary hair colorings contain similar ingredients as shampoos but in stronger, more concentrated form, leaving an even greater wax-like chemical build-up on the hair. Like shampoos, most hair conditioners contain plastic-derived polymers and petroleum by-products plus paraffin-like waxes. These so-called conditioning agents are designed to repair hair that has been damaged by the chemicals, such as ammonia, in permanent waves and hair colorings and by dehydration caused from blow dryers and curling irons. With frequent use, these chemicals and hair care appliances can melt the outer, horn-shaped layer of the hair shaft, and this is the major cause of tangles in hair. The paraffin-like waxes in most hair conditioners coat and seal the damaged hair cuticle at the base of the hair shaft. This glue-like coating gives a healthy appearance to the hair, but the effect is temporary and even more damaging. In addition to looking limp, over-conditioned hair appears dry and brittle, breaks easily, and is difficult to style and manage.

Nature offers us a healthy alternative for maintaining beautiful hair. Natural hair care shampoos and conditioning formulas can be created by combining the distilled essences of flowers and herbs with natural cold-pressed oils and the natural detergents derived from these oils. Shampoos made from these formulas have special cleansing effects because they loosen the deposits of glue-like synthetic chemicals that have accumulated over the scalp at the base of the hair follicles.

Similarly, cleansing and nourishing conditioners can be made from essential oils and the harmless wax-like polymers found in nature, such as those derived from wood products. These conditioners can repair damaged hair without causing build-up because they temporarily lubricate the hair and scalp and can be easily washed out in the shampooing process. Preparations containing essential oils are also helpful in promoting the growth of healthy looking hair because essential oils tend to penetrate into the scalp and stimulate the circulation of blood to the roots and hair follicles.

The best way to naturally cleanse and lubricate the scalp, we believe, is to use oils found in nature that resemble the body's natural oil, or sebum. The oil that we think is most like sebum in cleansing and lubricating the skin and hair is derived from the jojoba bean. For centuries jojoba has been used as a skin lubricant, and it is sometimes referred to as the youth or the wonder oil. Jojoba can be mixed with the oils of herbs such as lavender, sandlewood, or pettigrain to make hair conditioners that, for example, help protect against dry scalp and yet can be washed out in the next shampooing. Also, styling gels made from ingredients such as flax seed and aloe vera, which have excellent hair conditioning properties, have the same effect as synthetic gels but are completely natural.

There are many essential oil formulas that can be created to keep the hair healthy looking and to help prevent dryness, oiliness, and some types of scalp irritations. We recommend that consumers who want to use natural formulas always consult with and obtain these preparations from professional stylists who have knowledge and experience in the science of Aromatherapy.

An excellent way to cleanse and condition the hair and lubricate the scalp is to massage specially prepared formulas of essential oils into the scalp immediately before shampooing, when the hair is dry. The oils can better penetrate the hair shaft and the scalp when the hair is dry because oil and water tend to separate rather than to mix. Massaging these oils into the dry hair and scalp should be the first step in hair care, because it 1) loosens any deposits of glue-like synthetic chemicals which may have accumulated, 2) stimulates circulation to the scalp, and 3) helps nourish and balance, or condition, the hair and scalp.

The second step is to wet the hair thoroughly with a shampoo prepared from naturally-derived detergents, aloe vera, and herbal essences. (Herbs are beneficial in shampoos and conditioners only if they appear in the formula in large quantities and at highly concentrated levels. Most so-called herbal shampoos manufactured today contain a minimum of herbal ingredients, sometimes constituting as little as one-half of one percent of all the shampoo's ingredients.) The essential oils that were applied to the scalp in step one should now be massaged into the hair and scalp with water and the shampoo. Next, the hair should be thoroughly rinsed. This may be followed by another shampoo application and massage if desired. A natural astringent rinsing product may also be used at the end of the shampooing process. The acidic properties of rinses made with lemon or apple cider vinegar, for example, cleanse and condition the hair and scalp and help hair look and feel healthy and manageable.

Special precautions should be taken before any permanent wave or hair coloring solution is used on the hair. Permanent wave solutions contain thioglycolic acid and other synthetic chemicals that, we believe, if absorbed through the scalp and into the blood stream, have toxic effects. Hair coloring also contains strong chemicals that, if used in large quantities or over a prolonged period of time, may also be absorbed into the system. Therefore, we advise that the hairdresser or person applying a permanent wave or hair coloring be careful to apply these strong solutions only on the hair and not directly on the scalp. In addition, we recommend that natural oils known for their protective qualities (such as jojoba mixed with oils like sandalwood, lavender, or arnica) be massaged into the scalp before the permanent wave or hair coloring process. These oils, which must be combined in the right proportions, can help to prevent such chemical solutions from penetrating into the scalp.

Healthy hair is one of the most obvious symptoms of a healthy lifestyle. As we might expect, good nutrition and regular physical exercise are essential for the growth of healthy hair. While all types of physical exercise stimulate the circulation of blood to the scalp, there are two exercises that are particularly beneficial for the hair and scalp. The first is the headstand, which increases the flow of blood to the scalp. (See detailed descripton of yoga exercise, p. 80.) The second is a modified version of the headstand, known as the half-fish pose. To assume this posture, lie on a rug or mat and then arch the back, placing the elbows and forearms on the floor next to the body and gently touching the top of the head to the floor. Breathe diaphragmatically, smoothly and evenly, and hold this position for fifteen to thirty seconds. In addition to increasing circulation to the scalp, this exercise promotes deep inhalation by opening up the chest area. We recommend that all physical exercises be followed by several minutes of complete relaxation.

Aesthetics

THROUGHOUT HISTORY men and women have spent vast amounts of time, energy, and expense to dress and adorn themselves aesthetically. Archaeologists have found that the earliest tribal societies wore jewels, feathers, and skins of all kinds and painted, punctured, and even deformed the body to become what they thought was beautiful and to draw attention to themselves. In every age beauty has been interpreted differently; and society has always judged the degree of a person's success and attractiveness by what he or she wears and whether it conforms to the current standards of beauty. However, dressing attractively does more than give us social approval. Our manner of dress is one of the outward expressions of our thoughts and feelings. Dressing can be a creative opportunity for self-expression and can give us at least a temporary feeling of wellness and beauty.

Adorning the body with hairstyles, makeup, and clothing can be as creative as any other form of art. With the advent of shops that sell discounted and second-hand clothing, dressing stylishly can be relatively inexpensive. We believe that garments made of natural fibers, such as cotton, linen, and wool are the healthiest for the skin, which is the body's largest organ and needs to be properly ventilated. Unlike synthetics, natural materials allow the skin to breathe. As consumers, we should insist that clothing manufacturers provide us with more selections of natural fabrics.

Fashion is never static. It is an expression of the here and now, and what was wrong according to yesterday's fashion standards may be right today. Since "being young" means living in the present, we should wear up-to-date styles if we want to maintain a youthful appearance. By wearing hairstyles or clothes that most people wore ten years ago, we may be judged by society as being out of step. More importantly, we remain in the past and miss all of the enjoyment that accompanies change.

Inner Beauty

THE EXPRESSION "BEAUTY COMES FROM WITHIN" means that our outward appearance is the manifestation of how we see ourselves. At those times when our bodies are out of shape or our lives and relationships are out of balance, we may not feel at all beautiful. However, this feeling of unattractiveness can be changed by developing an awareness of our inner beauty.

Inner beauty need not be created, for it already exists in everyone in equal measure; and it is expressed in the gifts, talents, strengths, and potentials that make each of us uniquely beautiful. Rather than spending a lot of time, effort, and money on ways to improve our external appearance, we need to rediscover our inner beauty. This process involves finding and creating formulas for healthy living that will allow our natural beauty to surface. Perhaps the best sources of information about life, health, and beauty are people who, themselves, express their own inner beauty. These men and women can become our mentors, and the way they think, speak, and act can guide us toward rediscovering our own inner beauty and strength.

A technique that helps us recognize our own true beauty is called the positive mirror exercise. When most of us look in the mirror we see what is wrong or defective about our appearance. We mentally criticize those features that are not pleasing to us and worry about signs of aging. Even most internationally renowned beauties and famous models admit that at some time in their lives they felt like ugly ducklings. The mirror exercise is designed to help transform these self-destructive attitudes into self-awareness and self-appreciation.

The exercise should be practiced in a relaxed, positive frame of mind and in a quiet, secluded place where we cannot be disturbed. After bathing and when the hair is still wet, comb the hair away from the face. Stand before the mirror with the head, neck, and trunk straight and establish diaphragmatic breathing, inhaling and exhaling calmly, smoothly, and evenly. Begin by gazing into the eyes without blinking, and continue for as long as this feels comfortable. Soon we will notice a new freshness and beauty in our exterior features. By practicing the positive mirror exercise every day for a short period of time, we will begin to recognize and focus upon the best and most beautiful aspects of ourselves.

Practicing without clothing before a full-length mirror can also help us confront any need we may have to lose weight. We should practice self-affirmation, positive imagery, and eidetic and kinesthetic exercises to give us the motivation to begin dieting and exercising. (See Affirmation, Chapter 3.) This is one method of body transformation that does not require physical exertion but, instead, is based upon positive mental affirmations and resolutions. Practicing the full-mirror pose when the body is healthy and trim will reveal to us the unique beauty of our individual bone structure; and the self-affirming exercises will help us resolve to keep and enhance our health and beauty. Both the facial and full-body mirror exercises are extremely beneficial in creating and affirming a positive self-image.

Most of us think of beauty in terms of society's prevailing image of what is stylish or popular. Movie stars and singers often try to exemplify the current conception of "a beautiful personality." However, real beauty comes from who we are, from within, and not from someone else's image of beauty.

The art of being beautiful and living beautifully involves daily self-study of our interior and exterior selves. Through this lifelong process we will learn to recognize the inner beauty in ourselves and others.

1. I recommend using 7-10 drops of the Aveda L.D. Body Maintenance infusion (avoid eye contact).

6 *ACTIVITY AND TIME MANAGEMENT*

ALL OF US MUST BECOME MANAGERS OF LIFE. Just as running a successful business requires planning and management, living a healthy, successful life requires us to manage, or balance, our time and our daily activities. By using the techniques outlined in earlier chapters, we can select our goals and the mentors or teachers who can help us reach those goals. The next key to living successfully is proper management of time and space. The most common excuse is "I don't have time," and, in fact, there never is enough time and space to accomplish all of our goals. In this chapter we discuss ways in which to manage all areas of our lives, from our day-to-day economic and physical needs to our needs for mental and emotional growth.

Relationships

RELATIONSHIP IS THE CONSTANT ACTIVITY or interaction between the positive and negative (yin-yang) forces in nature and the entire universe. It is the phenomenon by which the earth, sun, moon, planets, and the entire solar system are connected. Similarly, we exist in relationship to the cosmos, to God, to plants, animals, and other human beings, t[...] material world, and to ourselves. This interaction bet[...] positive and negative is played out in our daily lives i[...] form of our attractions. We are attracted to people and things because they possess something that is missing within ourselves and we long to fulfill our inner needs and be complete or whole. In fact, the purpose of any relationship is to perfect and complete ourselves; and this is so because of divine design. Throughout life we continuously review the imperfections in ourselves and our surroundings and identify new ones. Only in relationship with someone or something else are we able to remove or counterbalance these imperfections. Therefore, all relationships are given to us for the purpose of self-perfection or self-growth. Unless we realize this truth, our relationships will not be as meaningful and as satisfying as they could be. On the personal level, male longs for female, and female longs for male; but our search for fulfillment also extends to the world of material objects where we long to satisfy our needs and our desires.

Each one of us carries in his or her subconscious mind an image or illusion of the perfect relationship and we are constantly involved in relationships in search of that ideal. Relationship problems are common in this society because we are impatient and expect instantly satisfying and perfect relationships. For example, a husband has his set of desires and expectations for "the perfect wife"; his wife's mind is similarly filled with desires and expectations for "the perfect husband." These expectations cloud the mind and cause it to become confused and ignorant of reality, or the truth. Such confusion is the hallmark of modern-day relationships. When we are attracted to someone as a potential partner or mate, subconsciously we might think, "This person may have something to offer; perhaps he or she resembles my ideal and can fulfill my desire for a perfect relationship." With these thoughts we begin to fall in love. If the other person does not immediately live up to our ideal or meet our mental "appointment," we become dis-appointed and love disappears as quickly as it appeared. This type of relationship is based upon illusion and not love. As long as our relationships are based on expectations and not reality, we will live in a state of fear, loneliness, and confusion. Love will continue to elude us because we are not searching for it; we are only looking for someone to satisfy our selfish expectations, which we mistakenly call love.

The law of cause and effect applies to relationships as to everything else. In fact, relationship means the constant interaction of causes and effects. Relationships exist everywhere: in the balance between alkalinity and acidity, yin and yang, and masculine and feminine. The mathematician finds a relationship in adding and subtracting, which is called mathematics. A chemist studies the causes and effects of alkalinity and acidity and calls the relationship chemistry. A husband and wife call their relationship marriage. The seasons refer to the relationship in nature between hot and cold or moist and dry months. There are hundreds of thousands of cellular relationships in our bodies, and they are part of a larger relationship between the body and the mind. The mind and breath function in relationship to one another, for when the breath is calm the mind is calm, and vice versa. Relationship means relating — relating to the truth, or reality, as it exists at this moment and relating to the world, each other, and ourselves in the lifelong process of being that leads us to the truth.

We become confused, disappointed or dis-eased when we fail to understand that cause and effect determines the substance of every relationship. How does cause and effect apply to our daily lives? The answer is that as we develop certain attitudes and cause certain events to occur, we shape our relationships and reap their fruits. Then why not learn to choose relationships that are helpful for us? It is said that opposites attract, but the laws of physics say that like attracts like. We carry into each relationship not only our image of the perfect relationship but also the composite of habit patterns, which has developed from our past experiences. Because each of us has different past experiences, we each have a different set of habits that shape our individual personality. Also, each of us has a different interpretation of truth and beauty and use different words to describe them.

Most of us are afraid that our personalities will crumble if we have to give up our interpretations of reality. Our truth is limited to our experience and is not the ultimate truth. Let go of the individual truth and allow the greater truth to be revealed. Let go of the fear of being wrong, as this fear shakes your whole reality, causing distortions. Masters of life realize that everything is like and is alike, because everything simply is. For them, subconscious fears evaporate and truth and knowledge replace all fears of the unknown. Because of our deep-rooted fears, we can become defensive and close-minded. This attitude is one of the biggest obstacles to creating successful relationships. In a happy, productive relationship there must be some common ground. Choosing relationships that are helpful to us means surrounding ourselves with people whose outlooks are, at least, somewhat similar to ours. For example, every day we have conversations that reflect what we believe to be true. Those around us cannot understand or even hear us unless they, too, have similar experiences and interpretations.

A person who understands and is experienced in the art of relationships is cautious about entering into them. He or she takes time to explore the other person's habits, ideals, and behavior and filter or assess that information before entering into a close relationship and becoming committed. This is a common practice in the business world. Successful companies conduct research on their future employees, getting to know their working background, education, personality, hobbies, and lifestyles. On the basis of this assessment, they determine whether or not the prospective employee will contribute to the company's growth and help the company accomplish its goals.

In the East, families often select mates for their children. Ideally, they compare a potential partner's family background, habits, personality, and goals with their own child's background and goals. For generations, children in the East have been raised to have immense love, respect, and commitment to their families and traditions. For this reason, marriages arranged by the parents and family can prove to be successful alliances. In the West, where traditions are young and the family structure is not as strong, children choose their own mates. This has meant, in many cases, that marriage is the result of our fear, loneliness and need for love, not a choice based on our understanding of the purpose of relationships. We fail to explore the other's personality and background before making our selection. We fall in love with our own expectations and illusions; and when the other person does not live up to them, or when his or her true personality surfaces, we separate. Our "appointment" turns to "disappointment" and hatred, and we become discouraged and fearful in all relationships. These unions fail simply because we did not take time to explore; and sooner or later we found that each other's habits were incompatible. To find healthy relationships for ourselves, exploration must be conducted patiently, observations must be filtered, and commitment must be complete. This is the best way to choose any relationship in life, whether it is a job, a place to live, or a mate. Finally, we should remember that no relationship is perfect. However, a relationship can become a true spiritual union if our goal is to enrich the relationship, rather than to satisfy our own selfish needs and desires.

The Importance of Change

OUR PLANET AND THE ENTIRE UNIVERSE are involved in continuous changes that occur in space and time. The motion or flow of change is so constant that we cannot escape it. Change is the process of growth, and it causes the cycle of births and deaths, the seasons in life.

We, as humans, tend to resist change because we have adopted certain habits and have become attached to them. We are afraid that, by giving up our habits, we will be forced to leave the safe, protective "comfort zone" that they provide. But change is inevitable, and resisting change is useless. Whenever we refuse to join in the flow of change, we are hanging onto the past. Resistance to change prevents us from being in the present, and soon we become disconnected with the here and now. Stagnation causes us to grow old because living in the past is aging. Some people believe that by keeping a certain style of clothing, hair, and make-up, they can remain young. Others in the business world may refuse to enter the age of computers and automation. Instead, they cling to outmoded methods, techniques, or machinery because they were successful in the past. These people fail to understand that youth means being in tune with the here and now. Youth is a state of mind that has nothing to do with the age of the body.

Those who refuse to participate in the present cannot understand today's world and will not be successful. In every age, society brings to us a new wealth of information. The Western world has moved into an age of processing data, or an age of information. Those who will become successful must have the latest information, and apply this information to their daily lives. They will become more aware of reality and more able to direct the cycle of cause and effect in their lives. One who is able to see the truth, or reality, for what it is and effect change is "successful." By ignoring this information or refusing to add to it, we resist the march of progress and limit our understanding of the here and now.

Unless we change, nothing will change for us. The best way to adapt to change and make it work for us is to conduct a daily analysis of cause and effect in our lives and develop strategies for changing. Only then can we forge a successful path through all of life's changes. There are two important steps in creating the pathway of change: 1) develop an attitude of desire and love for change, and 2) practice the skills necessary for change in all activities. After fully developing our desire and skills we will see the reality or truth. Let us explain it in this way: When we are afraid to do something, it is either because we have no desire or we have no skills. Say, for example, that we are afraid of public speaking. We will certainly have no love for public speaking if we are unsuccessful each time we address an audience. On the other hand, if our desire to learn is strong enough, we will regularly practice the skills needed in the art of public speaking. The more we practice the more skill we develop, until finally we reach a level of highly developed skills, or mastery. At this level we will have such a thorough knowledge of speech that we will understand its truth and speak with the conviction that only truth brings.

All fears can be overcome in the same manner. By developing desire and practicing and mastering our skills, we will attain the ultimate knowledge, or truth, for any activity in life. We call this the realization of practical, and not mere intellectual truth.

True knowledge
Activity: Practice, Skills
Attitude: Desire, Love

Economics, Business and Financial Growth

MONEY IS IMPORTANT, not because it can buy happiness but because it gives us independence. In turn, independence gives us mobility, and mobility allows us to search for and accumulate information and find mentors and teachers. Our information and our teachers can show us how the law of cause and effect operates in our lives.

Money can be seen as a form of energy. We use our skills daily in the workplace, where we are expending energy in a concentrated way for eight hours. We receive money for this expenditure of energy. Whoever pays us, whether an individual or a company, must also expend energy to make money to pay us. Therefore, money is an exchange of energy. The value of our energy is determined by demand. Society needs many valuable services to progress, and once we prove our value to society, there will be a need for our services or energy. If we have a speciality, if our skill level is high, or if the service is scarce but in much demand, a responsible society will pay us well for it. Gold is expensive because it is a rare mineral, and diamonds are valuable because of their purity and scarcity. If the energy that we contribute to society is pure and rare, we should be as highly valued as diamonds.

We are rich when we can give to ourselves and others and we are poor when we cannot. In other words, giving is expansion or reaching out. Every book of wisdom and all religions urge us to give to the poor. But how can we give if we, ourselves, are poor? It is our duty to become secure enough financially to help ourselves and others. It is also our duty to teach others how to sustain themselves, just as we, ourselves, have learned to be self-sustaining. A thief or a beggar should not be condemned but motivated and taught how to become self-supporting. If we took this duty seriously, we could eradicate much of the violence on our streets and reform our prisons. Reviewing and monitoring our finances daily ensures that we will be able to provide for ourselves and others. When our financial plans are not well-balanced we become stressed, anxious, and even ill at times. Financial security and growth can help us achieve mental and emotional balance, so balancing our bank account daily is part of balancing ourselves mentally.

Accumulating information and skills in the business world is essential, but just as important is the way we conduct business. Those who have no interest in becoming successful through selfless acts will never have rich, meaningful lives. Some people claim that they behave according to different values in their business and private worlds. Isn't it difficult enough to be true to ourselves without intentionally creating this split personality?

A successful business is simply a network of transactions in which everyone benefits. There are two ways to conduct business. One is to take advantage of others to enrich only ourselves and the other is to create successes for others so that they, too, can be enriched. A person who is wise and experienced in life chooses the latter course in all of his or her business and private relationships. The better we understand relationships, the more successful we will be in the outside (material) world and the inner (personal) world as well.

There are four basic principles in business, as in life. The first is the *creative principle*. This is the source from which everything in life originates. Just as mathematics creates numbers and chemistry creates formulas, creative ideas give birth to new businesses.

The second we call the *constitution principle*. Once a business, or anything else, has been created, we must give it order. We do this by setting goals and devising strategies and formulas to achieve those goals.

The third principle is the *governing principle,* whereby

regulations and procedures are established to govern the business, or whatever else we have created. These regulations and procedures sustain the business and give it stability. Religion and philosophy are codifications of the governing principle, because they were created to sustain and stablize humankind, through knowledge and ritual. Philosophy interprets life and tells us how to live. All the great books of wisdom have followed the governing principle by creating a philosophy of life.

The fourth is the *integration principle*. Once our creation is given an order or constitution and is governed by laws, we become one with it. We have sustained it for so long and identified with it so completely that we internalize our creation. At this point it is no longer our creation, but, instead, we belong to it. Let us use the following illustration: Three city employees are paving a street. The first person says, "I am working hard"; the second says, "I am working for the city to pave this street"; and the third says, "I am improving our city." It is the third individual who exemplifies the integration principle. John F. Kennedy encouraged us to have the same attitude when he said, "Ask not what your country can do for you, ask what you can do for your country."

Businesses excel first because the individuals behind them have achieved personal excellence. A corporation is successful because it has developed an excellent product that meets one of society's needs. Then it communicates information about its product widely. If others agree that the product is excellent, the product is duplicated or mass-produced. For example, fifty million McDonald's hamburgers are eaten each year because many people agree with the advertisements that McDonald's is a truly great hamburger. Similarly, Walt Disney's Micky Mouse character survives even after Disney's death because people all over the world see the character just as Disney created him: an endearing, comic version of ourselves.

The key to becoming successful in life or in business is to set long-term goals and devise a strategy for growth. The following practical suggestions help to structure and manage time so that all our goals can be reached.

A time-management diary or journal is essential. Journals can
be purchased or simply made from a loose-leaf notebook.

Goals: Page one of the journal should contain a list of
long-term goals, and beside each goal should be listed the date
for completion or achievement.

Activity delegation checklist: The next section of the journal
should be an activity delegation checklist. This is a list of tasks
we have delegated and the persons who will perform them.
Sometimes this list includes tasks we have delegated to
ourselves, and so the following suggestions should be applied
to ourselves as well as to others. Delegation is one of the most
important aspects of business and personal life because we
cannot accomplish all of our goals single-handedly. All of our
relationship skills come into play when we delegate authority.
However, delegation will not be successful unless the people
whom we ask to help us are committed to their assignments
and follow through to completion. Without their commitment, our goals will never be reached and we will become
disappointed. One of the major problems in delegation is that
the person who is assigned an activity may not hear or
understand his or her assignment. It is a fact of life that we all
hear selectively. We tune in to certain words or even to a tone
of voice and make our own interpretations of what is being
said. Often, this creates serious misunderstanding.

To prevent a negative outcome for any project, we recommend the following method of communication: 1) The person
delegating the activity, the *delegator,* should explain the task
clearly; 2) The person to whom the work is being assigned,
the *interpreter,* should be asked to repeat the instructions. If the
interpreter has properly understood the goal and the instructions, he or she will be able to paraphrase the delegator's
message. This ensures that both delegator and interpreter have
the same objective. 3) Write down the objective, the steps
involved, the deadlines, and any costs involved in what we call
a project commitment form. (See Figure 6.1) Both delegator
and interpreter should receive a copy of the form and should
review it often to see that the project progresses to completion.
These techniques save time by avoiding basic misunderstand-
ings that create extra work, and save relationships by avoiding
unnecessary stress and a waste of our emotional energy.

Calendars: In the third section of our time-management
journal we should list our major activities for the current year

**Project
Commitment
Form**

Project _____   Date _____
Requested by _____   Approval:
Assigned to _____   Dept Head _____
Purpose _____   Accounting Dept _____
                                       Other _____

Steps:	Dead-line	Cost	Commit-ment
	Final	Total Cost	

Date of invoice(s) _____
Terms of Payment _____

Other information _____
_____
_____
_____
_____

I, _____ , commit myself to complete the above project
by the agreed upon deadlines.

Signature   Date   Witness   Date

FIGURE 6.2:

Time wheels
(a) Daily time wheel
(b) Monthly time wheel
(c) Refer to your mental
    inventory list for
    goals and affirmations

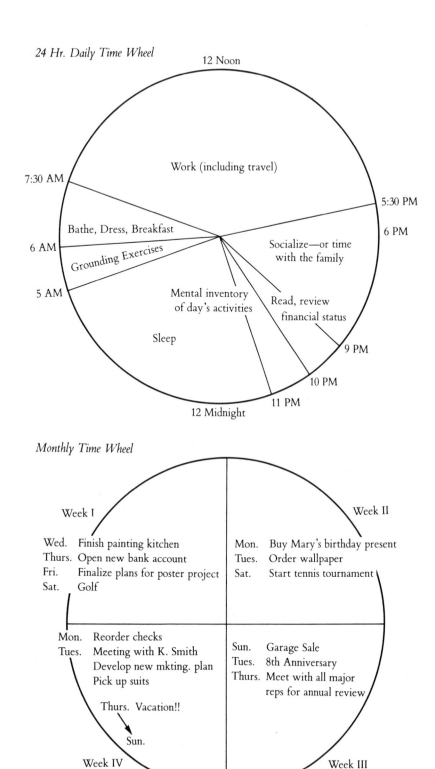

24 Hr. Daily Time Wheel

12 Noon

Work (including travel)

7:30 AM

5:30 PM

6 PM

Bathe, Dress, Breakfast

6 AM

Grounding Exercises

Socialize—or time
with the family

5 AM

Mental inventory
of day's activities

Read, review
financial status

9 PM

Sleep

10 PM

11 PM

12 Midnight

Monthly Time Wheel

Week I

Wed.   Finish painting kitchen
Thurs. Open new bank account
Fri.   Finalize plans for poster project
Sat.   Golf

Week II

Mon.   Buy Mary's birthday present
Tues. Order wallpaper
Sat.   Start tennis tournament

Mon.   Reorder checks
Tues. Meeting with K. Smith
       Develop new mkting. plan
       Pick up suits

Thurs. Vacation!!

Sun.

Week IV

Sun.   Garage Sale
Tues.   8th Anniversary
Thurs. Meet with all major
        reps for annual review

Week III

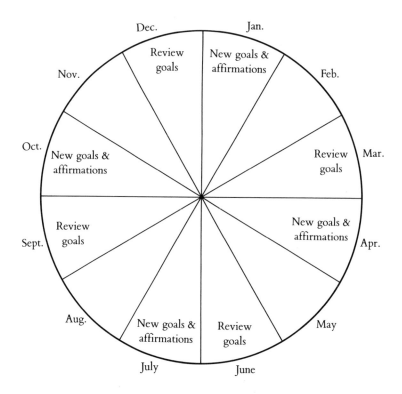

broken down into months. This is an overview of our strategic plan for the year. It should be followed by two more planning sections, the monthly and the daily calendar.

Resources: Another important part of our journal is the resource section in which we list information we need to accomplish our goals. For example, it might include notes taken from books, a list of reference materials, and so forth.

Finances: The financial section of our journal should be a picture of our overall financial health. By reviewing it daily, we can analyze the way in which cause and effect influence our existence on the material level.

Family: A family, or personal, section of the journal should include a schedule of important family activities, together with important dates, such as birthdays and anniversaries of our loved ones.

Meetings: In the next section we should record notes from important meetings and interviews. It is helpful to review these notes whenever we review or update our goals.

Directory: The final section in the journal should be a telephone and address directory of our business and personal contacts.

Another helpful device for time management is the ***daily time wheel.*** (See Figure 6.2) In this wheel we can divide our daily activities into time segments. For example, 5:00–6:00 a.m.: grounding and affirmation exercises[1] and physical exercise; 6:00–7:30 a.m.: bathe, dress, and eat breakfast; 7:30 a.m.– 5:30 p.m.: work and travel to and from work; 5:30–9:00 p.m.: socialize or spend time with family; 9:00–10:00 p.m.: review financial status and read (i.e., accumulate information); and 10:00–11:00 p.m.: mental inventory of the day's activities.

The time-wheel concept may also be applied monthly and yearly for planning activities and goals. Simply divide the time according to the importance of the activity and use the wheel as a reference. A similar wheel can be drawn to help us review our entire life's activities. Checking every six months on all activities (physical, emotional, mental, spiritual, material, and social), will tell us whether we are leading a balanced, healthy life that is conducive to growth and longevity.

Physical

PHYSICAL ACTIVITY TONES MUSCLE TISSUE, aides the circulatory system, and brings the entire body into balance. Exercise is one of the keys to maintaining a healthy body and a well-balanced mind. There are many ways to exercise the body (some of the most beneficial ways are discussed in Chapter 5). No matter what routine we choose, it should be practiced without causing the body stress or injury. Many of us go to extremes to create the perfect body. We spend far too much time admiring and attending to the body and forget all the other ways we can perfect ourselves. A healthy physical body is part of a successful life, but certainly not all of it.

Physiologically and psychologically the shape of the body has tremendous importance. If our body is out of shape, we will have negative feelings about our physical appearance. Obesity, for example, not only makes us feel unattractive, but modern medicine also considers it a disease that will shorten the lifespan. A well-proportioned body allows us to dress aesthetically; and appearance is important in today's hypercritical, competitive world.

From the time-management point of view, the best time of day to exercise is early in the morning, when the body is rested and fresh. The amount of time spent on an exercise routine depends upon our motivation. If we have sufficient desire or love for exercise and its benefits, we should spend one to two hours each morning exercising. Self-motivation and developing skills are the basis for enjoying any activity. So, too, physical exercise requires motivation and practice. Avoiding exercise may be due to one of the diseases or blocks in our attitudes described in Chapter 3 (Mental Cleansing), and if we have difficulty motivating ourselves to exercise, we need to examine our resistance. Exercise should be enjoyed, just as we enjoy a good meal, for both food and exercise nourish the body.

Spiritual

WE ARE HEALED in the spiritual domain. For perfect health and well-being, we should live in this world of balance and peace at all times. It is important to practice mental balancing techniques at regular times every day.[2] Daily practice will keep our minds free from mental toxins, or destructive thinking, and also free from the effects of the physical toxins that we ingest in impure food.

One of the favorite sayings of Swami Rama, a spiritual master who is living today is, "Live in the world, but remain above it." In other words, we should perform our duties in the world without becoming attached to them. Attachment creates dis-ease and manifests itself in our personalities as pride, possessiveness, anger, jealousy, greed, and sloth. By remaining unattached — living above the world — we can see ourselves interacting with cause and effect. From that summit we can learn how to be and how to become.

Endnotes

1. These exercises are described in Chapter 3.

2. These techniques are outlined in Chapter 3.

7 *THE FOUR INSTINCTUAL DRIVES*

HUMAN BEINGS ARE GOVERNED by the four primitive urges: food, sleep, sex, and self-preservation. Because food, sleep, and sex are all ways to maintain our existence, we can say that the fundamental drive is that of self-preservation. These four instinctual drives give rise to all of our desires. To satisfy these desires, we form habits; and the composite of all of our habits becomes our personality.

Use of Food

THE BIOLOGICAL NEED FOR FOOD is nature's way of ensuring that we receive sufficient nourishment to survive and grow. Our attitudes about food are formed, primarily, in childhood. Despite their best intentions, parents often instill in their children the fear that, if they are not well nourished, they will not grow. The concern parents have that their children are well-fed can have both positive and negative effects. Some parents unwittingly teach their youngsters to overeat. The habit of overeating can lead to obesity and even to serious illnesses such as heart disease and diabetes. Overeating can also cause major nutritional imbalances. Our modern diet of fast foods is sadly lacking in nutritional value. It is possible to eat large quantities of food and yet crave more. The real problem, of course, is that our diets are incomplete or unbalanced. (See Daily Physical Nutrition, Chapter 4.)

Another bad habit is eating to alleviate tension or stress. Because we subconsciously associate nourishment with our mother's love, we often try to mother our emotions by eating. When we feel hurt, neglected, or depressed, we often eat to soothe our feelings. In this way food becomes another escape from reality.

To overcome our self-destructive eating habits, we should observe all of our daily habits, for they tell us much about our response to stress. The techniques for self-observation, including the grounding exercise and the personal inventory, are effective tools for changing these self-defeating patterns. (See Grounding Exercise described in Chapter 3.)

Use of Sleep

SLEEP SHOULD BE A DAILY SOURCE OF REJUVENATION, but a variety of sleep disorders common to modern society often prevent the body from receiving the benefits of complete rest. For example, when we are tense it is difficult to sleep deeply, and disturbed sleep increases tension in life.

Sleep satisfies both physical and psychological needs. Those who suffer from depression, loneliness, and lack of purpose and direction in life tend to sleep too much. We all remember periods in life when the more we slept, the more tired we became. By contrast, those who live well-balanced and organized lives seem to need little sleep. There is evidence that some masters of life are able to lead long, rich, and productive lives with a daily average of only two-and-a-half to three hours of sleep. This is because they can control how quickly they enter the refreshing state of deep sleep. Clinical tests have shown that this is an unconscious state in which the mind experiences complete rest. Deep sleep is beyond the subconscious state in which dreaming occurs. The twilight, or dream state, is an intermediate level, which lies between consciousness and the unconscious state of deep sleep.

Most of us spend the majority of our sleeping hours reviewing the contents of the subconscious mind. However, masters of life can by-pass the dream level and immediately experience pure, revitalizing rest. They have so thoroughly mastered their physical, mental, and emotional lives that dreaming is unnecessary and even a waste of time, time better spent on other activities. We, too, can learn how to enjoy deep, restful sleep by organizing our mental lives — by regularly and systematically practicing techniques for mental cleansing and nourishing. (See Daily Mental Nutrition, Chapter 4.)

The *sleep exercise* is another helpful technique for falling asleep quickly and for enjoying sound sleep. It should be done at bedtime, after bathing and practicing the grounding, relaxation, and personal inventory exercises described in Chapter 3. Lie comfortably in bed and establish diaphragmatic breathing. Avoid any effort or strain and keep the breath even, smooth, and without jerks and pauses. In this exercise the exhalations should be twice as long as the inhalations, so you may count 2 breaths in and 4 out, 3 breaths in and 6 out, or whatever makes you feel most comfortable and relaxed. Using the two-to-one breath count, take eight breaths lying on the back, sixteen breaths lying on the right side, and thirty-two breath lying on the left side. Most people fall asleep before completing this exercise.

Use of Sexual Energy

THERE ARE MANY BOOKS ON HUMAN SEXUALITY, but the use of sexual energy is still one of the most widely misunderstood aspects of modern life. This misunderstanding can often be the cause of frequent separations and breakups that we experience in our intimate relationships today. It can leave us feeling depressed, and depression arrests the process of growth. By contrast, an intimate relationship that is well-balanced, fulfilling, and based upon love and respect can be enormously rejuvenating. Our sex life reflects our feelings of security and insecurity. Only when we understand these feelings by identifying their causes and effects can we enjoy all of life's pleasures, including sexual pleasure. If sexual experiences leave us feeling frustrated, we should avoid blaming ourselves and our partners. A healthier approach is to observe our own thoughts and activities patiently. Through the process of self-observation, we can learn from the past and improve the present.

Sex is not a pastime, game, or sport; neither is it a way to make others attached to us and dependent. It is a union between a man and woman in which the two can become one. When practiced with the proper attitude, it is a spiritual experience, a ritual, a form of worship, and an offering of love. All activities in life should be practiced with this attitude, and sexual activities are no exception. Unless we give selflessly in life we will not feel fulfilled, for giving selflessly is the key to happiness and inner fulfillment.

The sexual organs are designed for the purposes of reproduction and elimination of waste materials from the body. According to the ancient Eastern philosophies of yoga and Taoism, they are also part of a complex system of seven energy centers in the body. These energy centers, called *chakras* in Sanskrit, correspond to the major nerve centers, or plexus, located along the spinal column. The life force, prana or chi, which gives the body its health and vitality, originates at the lowest energy center, near the base of the spine. This life force is contained in the cerebrospinal fluid, which travels upward through the inside of the spinal colum. As the life force moves upward, it passes through seven major energy centers and, from there, through thousands of energy pathways called *nadis* in yoga, or *meridians* in the Taoist tradition. The four elements of earth, fire, air, and water, together with the five senses, are also associated with these energy centers.

This energy system is something like riding an elevator in a seven story building and visiting each floor. By stopping at each level, we notice that the inhabitants and the decor are different on every floor. Similarly, as energy moves upward through the body, it can become concentrated at any one of the seven energy centers; and each center manifests its energy with different personality characteristics. For example, the solar plexus, the center where food is "burned," is so named because it is associated with the sun or the element of fire. When our energy is concentrated at this center, psychologically we are concerned with obtaining the necessities of life, such as food, shelter, and clothing. The energy arising at this level of consciousness manifests itself as assertiveness and sometimes as anger and fear. As we might expect, the body's sexual energy is concentrated at the center of consciousness located near the genital organs, and this center gives rise to our sexual personalities.

ENERGY CENTERS Each of the seven energy centers, or chakras, also represents a different level of awareness, or consciousness, and it is possible to achieve balance, or mastery, at each level. Through many years of study and practice, some yogic and Taoist masters have expanded their states of consciousness until they have understood existence in its entirety. The following is a brief description of the seven energy centers and their functions.

Chakra 1

Root Center

Element: Earth
Perception: Smell
Color: Yellow
Shape: Downward triangle
Location: Coccyxgeal

This energy center focuses on the basic level of existence and is located at the base of the spine. Some of the issues it deals with are basic survival (life and death), safety, and jungle mentality (eat or be eaten).

Physical Area:	Function:	Symptoms of Imbalance:	Ultimate Balance:
Feet to knees	Solidity	Fear	Secure
Back of legs	Stability	Tension	Brave
Hips and thighs	Groundedness	Selfishness	
Hamstrings	Body consciousness		

Chakra 2

Pleasure Center

Element: Water
Perception: Taste
Color: Milky white
Shape: Connected triangles
Location: Prostrate

This energy center focuses on survival of the species and is located near the reproductive organs. Some of the issues it deals with are satisfaction, sexual and physical pleasure (good food, sex, and alcohol), beauty, and sensuality.

Physical Area:	Function:	Symptoms of Imbalance:	Ultimate Balance:
Pelvis	Hormones	Addictions	Satisfied
Front of legs	Flesh-libidinal	Fear of aging	Content with
Quadriceps	drive		self
Lower back			Faithful

Chakra 3

Energy Center

Element: Fire
Perception: Eyesight
Color: Red
Shape: Upward triangle
Location: Solar plexus

This energy center focuses on digestion and the distribution of energy throughout the body. It is located at the navel and some of the issues it deals with are ego, strength, personal power, aggression, and identity.

Physical Area:	Function:	Symptoms of Imbalance:	Ultimate Balance:
Abdomen	Burning fuel	Anger	Patient
Behind the	Digestion	Laziness	Energetic
stomach	Regulating	Insomnia	Assertive
Above the	chakras 1		Confident
navel	and 2		

Chakra 4

Heart Center

Element: Air
Perception: Touch
Color: Smoky gray
Shape: Intertwined triangles
Location: Cardiac muscle

This is the integrating center for the yin and yang of the upper and lower body regions. It is located in the space between the breasts and is responsible for processing emotions.

Physical Area:	Function:	Symptoms of Imbalance:	Ultimate Balance:
Chest	Nurture	Ungrateful	Compassioante
Heart	Purify	Hasty	Responsible
Breasts	Care for others	Talkative	Nurturing
Above diaphragm	Loving	Poor circulation	

Chakra 5

Throat Center

Element: Ether-space
Perception: Hearing
Color: Blue
Shape: Downward triangle
Location: Pharyngeal center

This energy center involves the creative aspect of the personality. Its purpose is to help motivate the creative process. This center is located in the throat and all creative processes originate here.

Physical Area:	Function:	Symptoms of Imbalance:	Ultimate Balance:
Hollow of throat	Expressing	Romantic crushes	Trusting
Neck	Talking	Idolatry	Devotion
		Creative block	Creative
		Rejection	Accepting

Chakra 6

Eyebrow Center

Element: Mind
Color: White
Shape: Upward triangle in circle
Location: Nasociliary nerve

This chakra is the center of intellect. It deals with the sense of intuition and conscious awareness. This center is located between the eyebrows.

Physical Area:	Function:	Symptoms of Imbalance:	Ultimate Balance:
Head	Rectify faults	Meanness	Wise
Forehead	in other	Lack of	Knowing
Eyebrows	centers	discrimination	Eyes to see
Medulla	Sensitive to	Philosophical	Discriminating
Pituitary gland	light	distortions	
		Lack of	
		awareness	

Chakra 7

Crown Center

Color: White, bluish-purple
Shape: Diamond
Location: Crown of head

This chakra is the spiritual center located at the crown of the head. Its main focus is spirituality and cosmic consciousness.

Physical Area:	Function:	Symptoms of Imbalance:	Ultimate Balance:
Cown of the head	Self-realization	Ignorance	Full spectrum
Above the head			

From the traditional wisdom of the East comes a wholistic perspective of sexual energy. Like all other energy, it is a manifestation of the life force; and like all other activities in

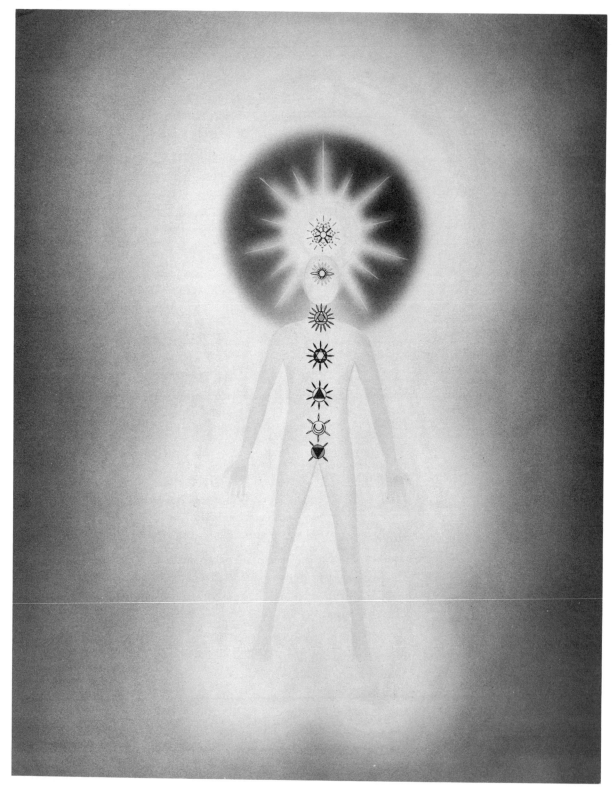

life, sex is a means for realizing life's purpose, which is union of self with the Self of all. According to ancient Chinese philosophy, everything in the universe is governed by pairs of opposites, yin and yang. These opposing energies, or poles, are continuously attracting each other to achieve balance, or oneness. Similarly, man and woman are attracted to each other in their search for oneness and fulfillment.

It is important that partners enter into the same mental state before lovemaking. We should feel deeply relaxed and peaceful and have thoughts of wellness for our partner. In this state of mind, or state of love, we should have no expectations but simply try to make our mind one with our partner's. The best preparation for lovemaking is to practice the grounding and diaphragmatic breathing exercises described in Chapter 3. The yoga exercises, if practiced regularly, also contribute to our ability to make lovemaking enjoyable for our partner and ourselves. Those with healthy sexual relationships have a positive attitude toward love and sex, and they avoid sexual fantasies and coarse language.

FIGURE 7.2:   Partner focusing

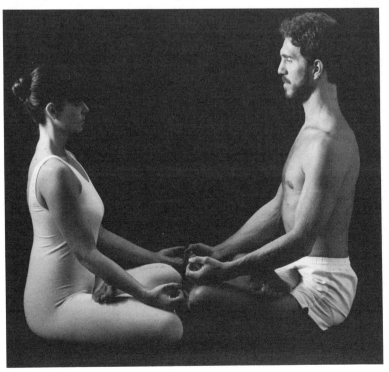

When our mind and the mind of our partner are in harmony, sexual activity can begin. To maintain sensitivity to our partner's needs, we should focus our awareness on the breath and consciously think about the loving nature of our union. The practice of diaphragmatic breathing is especially helpful in creating an even rhythm between partners. An uncontrolled breathing pattern is the sign of an inattentive mind. If we attempt any activity in life while we are mentally inattentive, we will lose control of our actions. The failure to remain aware of our partner's needs while making love may cause premature ejaculation of the male partner or the inability of the female partner to experience orgasm. If constant awareness and control of the breath is lost, lovemaking should stop, and the grounding and breathing exercises should be repeated. Love, patience, and commitment to our partner and to this practice as a form of worship can lead us to the highest levels of spiritual union.

Use of Self-preservation

SELF-PRESERVATION IS AN INNATE CAPACITY and as we continue to evolve through our life experiences it becomes a result of our environment, as well. The drive for self-preservation is the mother and father of all our primitive urges. It is so fundamental, in fact, that our attitudes toward food, sleep, and sex develop from the ways that we protect ourselves and cope with life. Each of us has a different approach to self-preservation, or a different set of defenses, based upon our unique life experiences. Our self-protective mechanisms sometimes clash with another person's, and this causes conflict in our relationships.

Fear is associated with self-preservation, and it is the greatest obstacle in life to overcome. All of our negative emotions originate from fear, such as the fear of not getting what we desire or the fear of losing what we have. Once the drive for self-preservation is redirected, we will no longer be self-centered and defensive. Instead, we will realize that by serving, preserving, and protecting our environment and others, we ensure our own self-preservation as well. A peaceful and creative life free from self-protective fears is the truest measure of success. The way to overcome fear and to transform self-preservation into a positive, healthy drive is to understand the purpose of life: By perfecting ourselves and serving others we realize that the individual self is one with the Self of all.

QUOTES FROM MASTERS OF LIFE

THE FOLLOWING ARE QUOTATIONS that have inspired me in my search for well-being:

We cannot change the world, but we can definitely transform ourselves. Self-transformation is essential, and not the reformation of the world.

SWAMI RAMA

If man is moderate and contented, then even age is no burden; if he is not, then even youth is full of cares.

PLATO

Blessed are the pure in heart, for they shall see God.

MATTHEW 5:3-8

If we cannot live for others, life is not worth living.

MOTHER THERESA

Lord, I cannot live without you.
You are the power behind my consciousness.
I love you.
Reveal yourself to me.

DAILY PRAYER, ANONYMOUS

Your self-existence is unchangeable, but your form is subject to change; the whole process of life teaches you that life is nothing but a series of changes. Beneath all these changes lies something that never changes. Grieve not, be aware of both.

SWAMI RAMA

Yoga is for everyone, for the West as well as the East. One would not say the telephone is not for the East because it was invented in the West. Through yoga, we can build a direct line to God.

YOGANANDA

Everywhere man blames nature and fate, yet his fate is mostly but the echo of his character and passions, his mistakes and weaknesses.

DEMOCRITUS

God can never be realized by one who is not pure of heart. Self-purification therefore must mean purification in all walks of life. And purification being highly infectious, purification of oneself usually leads to the purification of one's surroundings.

MAHATMA GANDHI

I will reveal to you a love potion, without medicine, without herbs, without any witch's magic; if you want to be loved, then LOVE.

HECATON OF RHODES

A pleasant and happy life does not come from external things; man draws from within himself, as from a spring, pleasure and joy.

PLUTARCH

We have everything necessary in the world today to bring about everlasting peace. It is only our selfishness that makes it impossible.

SWAMI RAMA

He who smiles rather than rages, is always the stronger.

JAPANESE WISDOM

Men are not worried by things,
but by their ideas about things.
When we meet with difficulties,
become anxious or troubled,
let us not blame others,
but rather ourselves,
that is: our ideas about things.

EPICTETUS

Teach us, good Lord, to serve Thee as Thou deservest; to give and not count the cost, to fight and not to heed the wounds, to toil and not to seek for rest, to labor and not to ask for reward, save knowing that we do Thy will.

ST. IGNATIUS LOYOLA

Our prayers will have power and wisdom.

YOGANANDA

Life does not need to be changed. Only our attitudes do.

SWAMI RAMA

Be not deceived; God is not mocked; for whatsoever a man soweth, that shall he also reap.

GALATIONS 6:7

There's only one corner of the universe you can be certain of improving; and that's your own self. So you have to begin there, not outside, not on other people. That comes afterwards, when you have worked on your own corner.

ALDOUS HUXLEY

Those who love the truth in each thing are to be called lovers of wisdom and not lovers of opinion.

PLATO

The more a person purifies himself or gets rid of his images, the nearer he is to God, who himself is altogether free of them. The more a man forgets his deeds, as well as the occasion of their performance, the purer he is.

MEISTER ECKHART

Close your eyes and you will see clearly.
Cease to listen and you will hear truth.
Be silent and your heart will sing.
Seek no contact and you will find union.
Be still and you will move on the tide of the spirit.
Be gentle and you will need no strength.
Be patient and you will achieve all things.
Be humble and you will remain entire.

ANONYMOUS TAOIST POEM

You are the architect of your life and you decide your destiny.

SWAMI RAMA

❦ *ABOUT THE AUTHOR*

THE AUTHOR, Horst M. Rechelbacher, born in 1941, grew up in an impoverished environment in Klagenfurt, Austria, just after the Second World War. The post-war conditions of malnutrition were so severe that, until the age of six, Horst and his family lived on a diet of coffee, cornmeal and bread. At the age of 14, he began to work in Klagenfurt as an apprentice in the beauty profession.

Through his natural talent and efforts, Horst soon gained a reputation throughout Europe as a master hairstylist and a leader in the beauty industry. In his teens and early 20's, Horst worked and taught in Italy, England, Germany, and France. At the age of 23 he came to the United States where he became a consultant and representative for many leading cosmetic companies. Horst has won every major hairdressing award worldwide including Intercoiffure's coveted Chevalier Award. Recently he was named the nation's super styler by a panel of fashion and beauty magazine editors. Horst is also a professional photographer. His hairstyles, photography, and writings are featured in top beauty, fashion, and health publications around the world. His art photography has been shown in a major New York gallery.

Horst had become an internationally famous trend-setter by his early twenties. He lived a jet-age lifestyle and used alcohol and stimulants as part of his daily routine. At the age of 28 he was suffering from a physical breakdown and deep psychological depressions, and it was then that he began searching desperately for alternative lifestyles that would lead him to physical and psychological wellness. During this search Horst met his teacher, H.H. Swami Rama, a renowned master in the yoga tradition. While studying with his teacher in India, Horst was introduced to a complete wellness-oriented approach to health and beauty, which included proper diet and nutrition, physical exercise, and positive thinking. Shortly after adopting these new lifestyle techniques the symptoms of his illnesses vanished.

Horst pursued his study of wellness, its origins in Eastern and Western science and philosophy, and its relationship to the essences and elements found in nature. Through his own studies and research, Horst has become one of the few authorities on Aromatherapy, the science of using the balancing and beautifying properties of specially selected essential oils, which are derived by distilling the absolute essences of flowers and herbs.

Horst's businesses have grown to include an internationally renowned chain of beauty salons and education centers and a cosmetic company with an international market. He founded the Aveda Corporation, which manufacturers pure and natural hair, skin, and body care products using the science of Aromatherapy. The principles of Ayurveda — the science of longevity — are applied throughout Horst's whole-body approach to beauty; and the whole, undiluted herbs which he uses as main ingredients, provided the basis for the product name "Aveda," derived from Ayurveda. Many of the body care products described in this book are available from the Aveda Corporation, 321 Lincoln Street NE, Minneapolis, MN 55413.

Horst's International Education Center for Hair and Esthiology (skin and body care) offers courses, including the complete study of physiological make-up (organ functions), the study of herbs and Aromatherapy, hair fashion (including cutting, coloring, and permanent waving), and clothing fashion. In addition, courses on complete skin and body care, therapeutic body wraps and massage, reflexology, polarity, and acupressure are also provided.

Many publications on wholistic health, exercise, nutrition, and yoga philosophy, as well as products such as the neti pot, which is used for nasal washes (see Chapter 3), are available from the Himalayan International Institute of Yoga Science and Philosophy, Box 88, Honesdale, PA 18431.

❦ SUGGESTED READING

Ayurveda and Aromatherapy

American Folk Medicine, Clarence Meyer, New American Library, New York, NY, 1973.

The Art of Aromatherpy: The Healing and Beautifying Properties of the Essential Oils of Flowers and Herbs, Robert F. Tisserand, Destiny Books, Rochester, VT, 1977.

Ayurveda: The Science of Self-Healing, Dr. Vasant Lad, Lotus Press, Santa Fe, NM, 1984.

Back to Eden, Jethro Kloss, Woodbridge Press Publishing, Santa Barbara, CA, 1975.

The Herbalist, Joseph E. Meyer, Meyerbooks, Glenwood, IL, 1918.

Homeopathic Medicine at Home, Maesimund B. Panos, M.D. and Jane Heimlich, J.P. Tarcher, Los Angeles, CA, 1980.

Homeopathy, Medicine of the New Man, George Vithoulkas, Arco Publishing, New York, NY, 1981.

The Patient, Not the Cure: The Challenge of Homeopathy, Margery Blackie, Woodbridge Press Publishing, Santa Barbara, CA, 1978.

The Practice of Aromatherapy, Jean Valnet, Destiny Books, Rochester, VT, 1978.

School of Natural Healing, Dr. John Christopher, BiWorld Publishers, Provo, UT, 1979.

Exercise

Exercise Without Movement, by Swami Rama, Himalayan International Institute, Honesdale, PA.

Hatha Yoga Manual I, Sanskriti and Veda, Himalayan International Institute, Honesdale, PA, 1985.

Hatha Yoga Manual II, Sanskriti and Judith Franks, Himalayan International Institute, Honesdale, PA, 1978.

Joints and Glands Exercises, by Swami Rami, Himalayan International Institute, Honesdale, PA, 1982.

Lectures on Yoga, by Swami Rama, Rudolph Ballentine, M.D. and Alan Hymes, M.D., Himalayan International Institute, Honesdale, PA, 1979.

Yoga for Beauty, Michael Volin and Nancy Phelan, Arc Books, New York, NY, 1971.

The Human Body

The Body Machine, Christian Barnard, Crown Publishers, New York, NY, 1981.

Chocolate to Morphine, Andrew Weil, M.D. and Winifred Rosin, Houghton Mifflin, Boston, MA, 1983.

Freedom from Stress, Phillip Nuerenberger Ph.D., Himalayan International Institute, Honesdale, PA, 1981.

Guide to Stress Reduction, L. John Mason, Peace Press, Culver City, CA, 1980.

Hand Reflexology: Key to Perfect Health, Mildred Carter, Parker Publishing, Englewood Cliffs, NJ, 1975.

Human Anatomy and Physiology, Barry King and Mary Jane Showers, W. B. Saunders, Philadelphia, PA, 1969.

Newsweek Encyclopedia of Family Health and Fitness, Kenneth N. Anderson, ed., Newsweek Books, New York, NY, 1980.

Primary Anatomy, John V. Basmajian, Williams and Wilkins, Baltimore, MD, 1976.

Science of Breath, Swami Rama, Himalayan International Institute, Honesdale, PA, 1979.

Shiatsu Therapy: Its Theory & Practice, Toru Namikoshi, Japan Publications, Briarcliff Manor, NY, 1977.

Nutrition

Diet and Nutrition, Rudolph Ballentine, M.D., Himalayan International Institute, Honesdale, PA, 1978.

Moosewood Cookbook, Mollie Katzen, Ten Speed Press, Berkeley, CA, 1977.

Recipes for a Small Planet, Ellen Buchman Ewald, Ballentine, New York, NY, 1973.

The Yoga Way Cookbook, Himalayan International Institute, Honesdale, PA, 1980.

Philosophy

The Greatest Miracle in the World, by Og Mandino, Frederick Fell Publishers, Hollywood, FL, 1975.

How to Get Control of Your Time and Your Life, Alan Lakein, New American Library, New York, NY, 1974.

The Management of Time, James T. McCay, Prentice-Hall, Englewood Cliffs, NJ, 1959.

Man's Eternal Quest, by Paramahansa Yogananda, Himalayan International Institute, Honesdale, PA, 1985.

Philosophy of Hatha Yoga, Pandit Usharbudh Arya and D. Litt, Himalayan International Institute, Honesdale, PA, 1985.

Success Through a Positive Mental Attitude, Napoleon Hill and W. Clement Stone, Prentice-Hall, Englewood Cliffs, NJ, 1960.

Yoga and Psychotherapy, The Evolution of Consciousness, Swami Rama, Rudolph Ballentine, M.D., and Swami Ajaya, Ph.D., Himalayan International Institute, Honesdale, PA, 1976.

Youth and Aging

Biology of Aging, Marion J. Lamb, Halstead Press, New York, NY, 1977.

How to Live to Be 100, Sula Benet, Dial Press, New York, NY, 1976.

Longevity, Kenneth Pelletier, Delacorte Press, New York, NY, 1981.

Los Viejos, Grace Halsell, Rodale Press, Emmaus, PA, 1976.

Maximum Life Span, Dr. Roy L. Walford, W.W. Norton, New York, NY, 1983.

The Methuselan Factors, Dan Georgakas, Simon and Schuster, New York, NY, 1980.

The Tao of Medicine, Stephen Fulder, Destiny Books, Rochester, VT, 1982.

❦ INDEX